Also by Jess Butterworth

Running on the Roof of the World
When the Mountains Roared
Swimming Against the Storm
Where the Wilderness Lives
Into the Volcano

For younger readers
The Adventure Club Series:
Red Panda Rescue
Tiger in Trouble
Polar Bear Patrol
The Orphan Orangutan

LOST ON GIBBON ISLAND

JESS BUTTERWORTH

Orion

ORION CHILDREN'S BOOKS

First published in Great Britain in 2023 by Hodder & Stoughton

1 3 5 7 9 10 8 6 4 2

A CIP catalogue record for this book
is available from the British Library.

ISBN 978 1 510 11032 8

Typeset in Mrs Eaves by Avon DataSet Ltd, Alcester, Warwickshire

Printed and bound in Great Britain by Elcograf S.p.A.

The paper and board used in this book
are made from wood from responsible sources.

Orion Children's Books
An imprint of
Hachette Children's Group
Part of Hodder & Stoughton Limited
Carmelite House
50 Victoria Embankment
London EC4Y 0DZ

An Hachette UK Company
www.hachette.co.uk

www.hachettechildrens.co.uk

To my mum, Anya

DAY 1

Midday

If you're reading this, hopefully you're coming to rescue me. My name is Lark. I'm twelve years old and I've been shipwrecked on an island. Writing 'shipwrecked' makes it sound as though I was washed up on an island by mistake, but I'm pretty sure it wasn't an accident. I think someone was trying to kill me. On purpose. In fact, I'm ninety-nine-point-nine per cent certain.

If someone doesn't find me soon, I'm going to send this notebook out in a bottle over the ocean to try and get help. And if help doesn't come in time . . . well at least you can use this diary as evidence for what happened to me.

You'll need to know where I am to come and rescue me, but the problem is I'm not sure I know. We started from mainland Cambodia in the boat early this morning, but we were on the boat for hours before it sank. I guess I'm on an island somewhere, but who knows which one.

It doesn't seem like there are any other humans here. There are no roads, buildings or sounds of human life.

After the boat sank and I was washed up on the rocks, I climbed over them and forced my way through thick jungle until I found this beach. All I can see from here are foaming waves stretching out to the sky in front of me and dark impenetrable jungle behind me. I'm working up to venturing back in there to explore.

What else is there that might help you figure out where I am? Well, to either side of this beach are rocks and cliff edges. Huge waves hammer against them. Earlier I stood at the rocks and watched, counting the seconds between the waves, wondering what my chances of climbing down from one rock and up on to the next were so that I could explore beyond them. I never got past two seconds. Not enough time to avoid being trapped by the crashing waves.

All of that means that, for now, I'm stuck here.

If you're wondering how I'm writing this, I found a washed-up purple felt tip pen in the sand, and it works! I already had my notebook. I knew I'd have to wade into the sea to get on the boat this morning, so I'd packed my notebook in a waterproof zip bag and shoved it in my pocket and it somehow survived with me.

If only I'd known what was about to happen, I'd have filled that waterproof bag with so many more things. Still, at least I have the notebook, I guess. And there's all sorts of bits and bobs that have been washed up on the beach. Later, I'll look for a biro or a pencil in case this pen runs out. I know there are other things I should be doing too, but to tell the truth . . . I'm scared. Every time I look up from this notebook the vastness of the sea stretches in front of me and I feel more alone than I've ever felt before. I have bruises and scratches all over my body, but I haven't felt the pain yet – my mind is moving too quickly, thinking about everything else.

I need water and food and shade from the sun. I need to make a flag or a sign – something that any rescue boat or helicopter could spot from far away. There's so much I need to do – but I just can't get myself to move. Dad's voice is in my head, telling me to make sure I drink water when it's hot. That's what I'm going to do first. Find something to drink. I'll come back to writing this soon. Wish me luck.

Afternoon

I'm back from my search along the beach for fresh water. I didn't get very far because the scorching sand burned the soles of my feet. I had to keep ducking into the shade of the treeline, or out into the sea, to let my feet recover. I didn't find any fresh water, but I collected a bunch of other things, and now I have a little pile of items next to me.

Things I've found so far:

- A coconut (Not as great as that sounds. More on that in a minute)
- Seven empty plastic bottles
- Nine plastic bags
- Rope
- Broken fishing net
- A fishing buoy
- A yellow Lego figure

Weirdly the Lego figure was the thing that made me want to burst into tears. It's similar to one of my little brother's. Olly. It was only this morning that I saw him, fast asleep back in the hotel on the mainland. How can he be so near yet so far away at the same time?

I keep glancing at the plastic bottles and wishing there was lemonade in them. Or water. And now I've started thinking: if I have to send this notebook out to sea in a bottle, what kind of bottle should I choose? I've always imagined a glass bottle with a cork in it, but how likely am I to find one of those?

The coconut is in front of me. If I shake it, I can hear liquid sloshing about inside of it. I thought I was saved from dehydration when I spotted the palm tree and saw the brown furry coconut poking, half buried, out of the sand below it. *Yes.* I crawled on my hands and knees and snatched it and bashed it against a rock, but nothing happened apart from a small chunk flying off and hitting my leg.

It turns out the coconut water is trapped in a shell made of a thick fibrous husk. I have absolutely no idea how to open it. I've tried bashing it against the rocks. One end has a slight dent in it which I've attempted prodding with a stick. None of it has worked.

Now I've used up the last of my energy and I have absolutely nothing to show for it. The coconut is just *there*, taunting me, and every time I swallow it's like sand sliding down the back of my throat. I'm trying to remember the last time I had water. It must have been in the early hours of this morning, before I said goodbye to Mum. It feels like that was days ago. It seems bizarre that I'm surrounded by water but I can't drink it. I remember back at the hotel, Dad telling me it was dangerous to drink sea water. I can't remember why. It's too salty, maybe?

I'm perched on the sand at the edge of the jungle where there's shade. Crabs are darting across the beach in front of me and I can hear a toucan swooping through the leaves above. I've tried napping but I can't fall asleep. I'm too wired. And hungry. And sore. And thirsty.

I need to take my mind off it all. If I'm going to send this diary out as evidence, I have to explain more about what happened to me. I'd better start with the important things while I still have some energy. It's all floating around in my brain like parts of the wrecked boat. I wish I could piece it back together.

First things first. If you do find this notebook, can you look for my family and tell them I'm alive? My mum is called Erin Robertson, my dad is called Jasper Grey, and my little brother is called Olly Robertson-Grey. My mum shouldn't be too hard to find. She's a journalist. An environmental journalist, to be precise. Her job is what brought us to Cambodia in the first place. She had been asked to investigate disappearing gibbons from Cambodia's north-eastern forests. I remember her face the day she burst in to the living room to tell us. All smiles and eyes shining with excitement. She had lifted Olly up and spun him around in the air.

I feel guilty now because I wasn't excited at all when she told us. My best friend, and acrobatic gymnastics partner, Sophia and I were about to compete in a competition together. We'd been practising for months, balancing on each other's shoulders and tumbling across the floor, perfecting the routine to a piece of piano music that Sophia had found. The piano music sounded like a cascading waterfall and at our last practice I pretended I was a water droplet as I leapt off of Sophia's shoulders and twisted through the air, landing perfectly. If I close my eyes and breathe in deeply, the sound of the sea takes me right back there.

It's hard to remember that day and everything that followed – I can't help but feel like it's my fault I ended up here alone – but I need to tell you everything. I've always doodled whenever I'm trying to remember something uncomfortable. It helps get me ready to think. My favourite doodle is a lark. I've drawn them since I was little. Here goes . . .

Later that same day, Mum told us her news. I realised in that moment that I wouldn't be competing in the competition, but instead travelling across the world for Mum's job – again. That's the thing about Mum's job.

It always comes first.

'There will be more gymnastics competitions,' Mum said. 'But there might not be any gibbons left soon.'

'Why do *I* have to go?' I asked. 'I'm sure that I could stay with Sophia. You know her parents.'

'Oh sweetheart, this is such a great opportunity for you,' she said. 'You'll learn so much. I know you will. I want to show you Cambodia. I fell in love with it and the gibbons there when I visited in my twenties.'

I remember how I ran up to my room, biting back tears and throwing my head under my pillow. She didn't get it. She'd never even been to one of my competitions. She was always working on something.

Mum followed me in and sat down next to me on the bed, speaking softly. 'I know it's difficult, Lark. But I need to stand up for what's important and for what I believe in. One day, you'll find something that you really care about and then you'll understand why this matters so much.' She rubbed my back.

I wanted to tell her that I'd already found something important and that it was this competition, but I stayed silent and squeezed my eyes shut.

Mum sighed and kissed the back of my head before leaving.

I doubt having to survive on a desert island was what Mum had in mind when she'd said that I'd learn so much by visiting Cambodia. Still, I'm trying to stay as positive as possible. One good thing about this whole mess is that I'm certain Sophia will forgive me for missing the competition once she finds out. When I'd told her, she'd said she wasn't mad, but her face had crumpled and, as she'd looked away, tears had dripped down her cheeks. I'd let her down. And there was nothing I could do about it.

That was the worst thing. But you can't stay mad at someone after they've been lost on a desert island, right?

My purple felt tip is already running out, but I've got so much more to explain. I'll see if I can find another pen.

Half-moon, dusk

I haven't found another pen yet but this one is still working for now. I've had a second go at opening the coconut but no luck. I have to say, I thought a search party would have been sent out and found me by now. It's almost dark.

The moon rises early here, during dusk. I'm not going to be able to see anything soon. The sun was so strong during the day I kind of forgot that eventually it would go down and then night would begin. What do I do now?

There's another thing; the jungle here

screeches as it gets dark. It sounds almost like babies screaming and when I first heard it I turned and ran towards the shrieks. But once I was in the trees, the cries surrounded me, coming from all directions. The screams rang out in different pitches over the thrum of cicadas. As I turned around and around, trying to work out where they were coming from, a huge frog leapt in front of me and I jumped and ran as fast as I could back to the beach. I think it's the frogs screeching. I had no idea that frogs can sound like screaming babies. It reminds me of how goats sound human when they scream. Sophia showed me a funny video of them once. The frogs aren't funny but it's a whole lot better to have screaming frogs than a haunted jungle, right?

There's no way I'm going back into that jungle. Who knows what other creatures lurk in there? I can't remember whether there are big cats here in Cambodia. Or snakes? Scorpions? Bears? Wolves? I'm certain there's at least one thing that might eat me so I'd rather take my chances on the beach.

My writing's getting a bit scribbly. To be completely honest, when I started writing this, I didn't really think I'd have to send out this notebook in a bottle. It started out as something to fill the time until I got rescued, something cool I could show everyone when I went back to school. But now . . . well, I don't know. I'm beginning to doubt that I'll make it off the island by nightfall. And maybe . . . maybe I won't get rescued at all. No one knows where I am, and I'm not sure how much longer I'll be able to stay alive here without water.

If anything happens to me, there's some more things that you need to know. Lives depend on it.

The first important thing for you to know is

that there were three of us on the boat. Me, Vanna and a gibbon. I lost Vanna as soon as the boat sank. I don't know if she made it. I hope she's here somewhere, washed up just like me, but I haven't seen any sign of her.

The baby gibbon made it, partly because of some super strength I didn't know I possessed. It's not easy to think about but I'll try my best.

The whole time I was in the sea I managed to keep the gibbon with me, clutching on to her small body and pushing her above water as the waves washed over us. Even as she scratched and bit at my fingers to get away, I held on. If I had let go she would have drowned. By the time we washed up against the shore, she'd run out of energy. I cradled the limp gibbon as I clambered on to the rocks of the island, even though I was shaking and spluttering and coughing. I held on to her through the jungle, right up until I tripped and that was the moment my super strength disappeared . . . and the gibbon slipped from my fingers. She dropped to the ground and rolled over tree roots and down on to the beach.

I was scared to look and my heart pounded, but I forced myself to run after her. I couldn't have brought her this far just to lose her the moment we made it to land. I raced up to her lying crumpled and motionless on the sand. A tiny black furry body with golden cheeks.

I lifted the gibbon up gently. I thought I felt her breathing as I laid her in the shade on the sand. I knew how to perform CPR. Mum had said it was important to learn. But would CPR work on a gibbon? She was so small. I didn't want to hurt her.

'Please don't be dead,' I whispered. I remember my words being whisked away on the wind.

Luckily, right at that moment, the gibbon spluttered, opened her eyes and looked at me.

'Oh, thank goodness,' I said.

And then the most amazing thing happened.

The gibbon climbed into my arms and wrapped her four long fingers around my index finger and squeezed, as if to say thank you. She looked up at me with big dark eyes. I stayed very still. But then she spotted the trees and let go of my finger. The gibbon threw her long arms into the air above her head and ran into the jungle on two legs. As soon as she reached the low branches, she swung up in to the trees.

'Don't go,' I said softly.

The gibbon didn't look back. She climbed higher and higher.

'Please,' I said. The sound got caught in the back of my throat. 'Please don't go. Don't leave me here alone.'

I even tried to chase her through the thick

jungle but she disappeared up into the trees. I made noises with my tongue as if I was enticing a cat down but she didn't come back. The jungle was silent except for the wind and the birds. My heart sank. There was just me. I'd never felt so lost and alone.

So if you're reading this, it's not just me you need to come and save. It's the gibbon and Vanna too.

Night

I've been searching for Vanna. The darkness brought waves of panic and I dashed up and down the beach, shouting her name. I scrambled and climbed up rocks to get a better view. I stared out over the waves, which were space-blue and endless, with white foam illuminated by the half-moon on the top of them. I screamed as loudly as I could. I couldn't see any boats or any other land for that matter.

'Help!' I shouted. 'Anyone?'

But the only answer was the flutter of birds being disturbed, alongside the roaring wind and waves.

Now I'm here, collapsed on the sand. It looks like I'll be here all night. At least it's not cold. I can hardly see to write now, even with the moonlight. It's so dark here, and there's not a single sign of human life.

DAY 2

Dawn

It's morning and I'm alive. Barely. The sun isn't fully up yet, but there's just enough light to write by so I'll try my best to tell you what happened last night.

My dreams were filled with images of water. Of drinking it and swimming in it, of quenching my thirst and drowning at the same time. It was a sound that lifted me from my nightmare. A loud squeaking sound, piercing through the air.

My eyes snapped open. I wondered if I'd imagined it. It was still pitch black then.

The first thing I realised was that I was completely covered in itchy bites. I brought my fingers to my face and touched raised bumpy spots.

It took a few seconds for my eyes to grow accustomed to the dark. I sat up, looking all around me. The squeaking sounded again. I recognised it. The gibbon. Maybe she was injured after her fall. Did she need my help? Shadows twitched around me. I looked into the dark jungle but didn't see the gibbon.

With my eyes adjusted, and the moon peeking out from the clouds, I saw movement on the trunk of the tree that I was sleeping under. It wasn't the gibbon though. It was a snake. A *big* snake, slithering towards me.

My scream caught in my throat as I crawled backwards over the sand away from it.

I stopped when I reached the entrance to the jungle and scrambled to my feet, shrieking as I sensed more movement above me. But it wasn't the snake this time; it was something small and furry with two big eyes. The gibbon. She let out her warning squeak two more times.

The gibbon jumped on to a tree deeper in the jungle. I panicked for a second that she was leaving me again. But then she stopped and looked back, as if waiting to see if I'd follow her. I walked tentatively into the protection of the trees, knowing it wasn't safe on the beach but not feeling much safer in the jungle. There were still so many noises. Cicadas hummed and frogs screeched around me but there were other animal noises I didn't recognise, and those made me shudder.

The gibbon paused on a tree with low branches. She waited until I was directly underneath, then climbed higher before stopping and staring at me again.

'You want me to come up there?' I asked.

The gibbon tilted her head at me.

'OK,' I said. 'I'll try.'

I jumped and caught a branch and pulled myself up. The gibbon made a quieter squeak, as if delighted that I'd joined her in the tree. She turned and swung higher and higher.

I climbed quickly at first, but soon the branches thinned and creaked beneath me so I slowed down, carefully testing each branch with my weight before heaving myself up. One bent and snapped when I grabbed it, nearly sending me tumbling through the canopy to the ground.

'I can't go any further,' I shouted after the gibbon. 'The branches are too thin.'

The gibbon paused for a moment, then climbed down closer to me. She sat upright on a fork in the branches above my head, leaning her back against the trunk, and closed her eyes. I glanced around me and manoeuvred on to the widest part of the branch where I felt balanced. There was no way I'd be able to sleep here like the gibbon though. I'd fall out of the tree. I snapped thinner branches off and built a barrier, almost a nest around me. I leant against the trunk like the gibbon, trying to get comfy. The night wasn't too cold but I shivered. After a while, the gibbon climbed down and on to my legs before nuzzling into my chest and the nook of my neck. She snored softly as she slept.

'I'll get us off this island,' I said, stroking her soft fur. 'Don't worry, I'll help us.'

Her fur smelled of leaves and musk. It was fully dried now and fluffy.

'I wonder what your name is?' I asked. *Goldie* popped into my mind, because of her golden cheeks and how precious she was. 'Do you like Goldie?'

The gibbon let out a big snore and I smiled. Goldie the gibbon it was.

I didn't sleep the rest of the night. I kept thinking that I was going to tumble out of the tree. But it didn't matter because I had Goldie with me and I knew that together we'd make it through the night. Everything would be OK in the morning.

And we *have* made it through the night. I'm exhausted but she's sleeping soundly on me and the first rays of light are beginning to shine through the trees. I couldn't be more relieved.

Sunrise

I must have drifted off for a few minutes. I've woken up and Goldie is gone.

Early morning

I found Goldie again high up in the trees above me. Actually I heard her before I saw her.

The first thing I heard was a strange sound, a bit like a squeaky howl. Then came other noises. One that sounded like a fire engine and then an operatic twittering. It didn't resemble any bird I'd ever heard before.

That's when I realised it wasn't a bird, it was the gibbon, perched high in the tree, singing her heart out. Her black fur glistened and the yellow morning light made her golden cheeks glow.

Her song reminded me of a story Mum often told me, about how she chose my name. Apparently, when she was pregnant with me, larks would sing over her head – no matter which country she was in as she travelled through Europe for work.

I was stiff and thirsty, but I still wanted to sing with the gibbon. I pursed my lips and tried to whistle, to see if I could make the same sound. At last, I managed it. Our duet rang out over the trees. The wind carried the song notes into the sky. It filled me with hope, and all my panic from the night lifted.

I know we're going to get off this island. I can feel it in my aching heart. We have to.

I've climbed down from the trees, sore and cold, and limped on to the beach. As I've been writing this, my muscles have warmed in the light of the sun. I feel like a fern unfurling in the warmth as I stand. I scratch my scalp and my back. My body is covered head to toe in itchy red bites. Sandflies. They swarm around my ankles if I stand in the same bit of sand for too long. I hate them. A crab darts sideways over my toes and I leap on to a piece of driftwood.

If I thought I was thirsty yesterday, today it's even worse. Even my eyeballs feel dry.

Early morning, still

I've just done a wee in a bottle because I had a sudden idea that maybe I could drink it. The wee was the colour of Mum's cup of tea

28

before she puts the milk in. Does that mean I'm going to die soon? Either way, I'm definitely not drinking my wee.

The stupid coconut is still there, taunting me. I've even found another one and I bashed it with a stick until I was too dizzy to keep going. I've actually discovered a whole tree with green coconuts clustered at the top of it, but I can't even get to them, let alone open them up. And all the time the sea water is right there, looking cool and thirst quenching. Just one sip. How bad can it be?

late morning

It turns out that drinking sea water can be *very* bad. A few minutes after I tried drinking some, I was doubled over, retching. My stomach twisted and lurched. The smell of vomit and bile surrounded me. Fish swam up to the surface to eat my floating vomit which made me puke again. I splashed cold water on my face and body and shakily limped to the shelter of a tree, making sure there were no coconuts overhead that could fall on me.

That's where I am now, curled up in the sand. I want to cry but I don't even have enough moisture left in me to do that. I squeeze my eyes shut and wish that this would all be over, but when I open them, I'm still here. I remember the sandflies and now I really am crying.

I've found a big palm frond to lie on. At least that should protect me slightly from the sandflies.

Soon I'll go and search for water again. That's the most important thing to do. I just need to rest a bit first.

I can still smell my vomit and it's reminding me of our journey to Cambodia. It was one of the last times we were together, all four of us. I keep thinking the more I write down, the more I'll be able to piece together what happened. So here goes . . .

It took two flights and fifteen hours to get to Cambodia and Olly threw up in the first thirty minutes of our first flight, to the other passengers' horror. We had such a quick aeroplane transfer time that we couldn't shower him at the airport stopover. Even though Mum and Dad attempted to clean him the smell just wouldn't disappear. When the second flight landed there was a rush to leave the plane.

'Let's wait until everyone's off,' Dad said as I stood up.

Dad carried Olly. Me and Mum had bags hanging off us as we disembarked, stepping down steep metal steps on to the landing where a bus was waiting for us. I remember the first thing that hit me as we stepped off the plane was the air – it was hot and humid and heavy, no wind at all. The sky was a deep blue.

Olly groaned at the sight of the shuttle bus. 'It's OK,' Dad said to him. 'We're almost there. You've done so well.'

As we drove in a taxi from the airport to the coast, we passed through a big city, driving by skyscrapers, square buildings and temples with pointy gold roofs. Washing hung on balconies and monkeys slid down overhead power lines. Buses, cars, rickshaws, motorbikes and bicycles weaved in and out of each other along the road. It's odd to think of that busy city when I'm here on this empty island with no one else around. It feels like another world.

I remember complaining that I was starving. My hunger then was *nothing* compared to how hungry I am now. I vow to never say I'm starving again – if I ever get out of here.

I can still taste that meal we had together as if I was right there. Mum suggested getting breakfast noodles and the driver pulled over. We sat down outside on plastic chairs to eat them, next to the big leaves of a banana tree. I slurped up the thin rice noodles in soup. It tasted of coriander and spice. I'd do anything to have a bowl of those noodles now.

At the table I caught sight of a blue and red spotted gecko on the tree trunk opposite us and tried to get Mum's attention but she was on the phone talking to someone about work and shushed me. I remember feeling annoyed that she'd forced us to come here as a family and didn't even have time to *be* a family.

Back in the taxi, we passed a museum with a red skull and crossbones picture in the window. A big sign saying 'Welcome to the Landmine Museum' hung over the entrance with some Cambodian written above it.

'What does that mean?' I asked, purposefully directing my question to Dad.

Mum answered anyway. 'Cambodia still has many unexploded landmines.'

'I thought you said it was safe here,' I said accusingly.

'There won't be any where we're going,' said Mum. She turned to me and Olly. 'But you can't wander off, OK?'

I nodded stonily.

Mum continued, trying to engage me in conversation. 'I read an interesting story about how they're using rats to find the unexploded mines because they have an amazing sense of smell and they're too light to set off the mines.'

I did want to know more about the rats, but instead I looked away out the window, not ready to forgive her yet.

Back on the beach, I stare at the empty spaces either side of me. I hope there are no landmines on this island. I don't even know if this island's still in Cambodia. I wish I could get back to that day of us all being together as a family, even if it meant smelling of vomit.

Mid afternoon

I'm thinking about sending out this notebook in a plastic bottle today, unless I find water soon. I wanted to finish explaining how I ended up here first, so whoever finds this has the best chance of rescuing me, but it's only day two of being here and all my energy has been zapped away already. It's worse than that really. I don't even feel thirsty any more but my heart races, faster than usual, all the time. When I stand up I feel as if I'm about to faint. My lower back aches painfully on the inside. It terrifies me to write this but I don't think I'll make it another day without water.

Goldie has been watching me through the trees all day. I keep seeing the flash of her golden cheeks through the shadows. I wonder if *she's* found water. My skin is blistered and burning from the sand. It's too hot to walk on. I have to construct some makeshift shoes so I can try and search for something to drink.

I'll be back.

I'm now the proud owner of plastic bag shoes. Seven layers work surprisingly well against the heat.

late afternoon

I feel amazing! You'll never guess what I did.

I opened the coconut.

I found some plastic stuck in a crevice between two rocks at the cliff edge. It gave me an idea. I prised the rubbish free and then wedged the coconut between the rocks, making sure it was firmly stuck. Then I dropped a heavy rock on top of it. I heard a crack and the top part of the coconut came loose. I almost passed out lifting the rock but then I was able to peel away the husk and get to the shell, which was split open. I carefully pulled the top half of the coconut away and tipped the bottom half up to my mouth and drank the sweet liquid inside. I even used the bit that had smashed off as a spoon to scoop out the coconut flesh and ate that. It was the best feeling ever.

There was only a gulp of liquid inside, but it was something.

I gathered the other three coconuts I had found on the ground and opened them the same way. And now I'm not going to die. At least not today.

The coconut water didn't totally quench my thirst but it gave me enough energy to walk along the beach and scavenge more things that had washed up.

Today I've got:

- Nine more coconuts
- More plastic bottles
- Plastic bags
- Some tangled rope
- A red rag
- A ripped blue T-shirt that I'm using as a hat
- Two more pens (which is lucky because the one I was using is officially out of ink now)

When I first saw the T-shirt, for a split second I thought that it was Vanna, lying still in the sand. My stomach somersaulted and I dashed over to it, screaming her name. But it was just a blue T-shirt, and it wasn't even the same colour as the pink and white tie-dye one she'd been wearing the day our boat sank.

I should tell you more about Vanna, so you know what she looks like, because she might need rescuing too. It's hard to focus. Even after drinking the coconut water, I'm still so thirsty. And hungry. But I'll try and write down everything I remember about her.

The first day I met Vanna, I was with Mum, Dad and Olly. It was a few days after we'd arrived at the hotel. Mum's friend Bora was supposed to be meeting us that morning. Mum had told me a bit about him over lunch. He ran a fleet of tourist boats but had become concerned about the missing gibbons – he knew Mum from years ago and had asked her to help.

I can picture the beach we were on then, lined with hotels and cafes. We were sitting at a table with a huge parasol that protected us from the sun. Laughter filled the air as other people played and jumped in the waves. On our table

stood drinking bottles filled with fresh water
and tall glasses of mango juice.

Mum chattered excitedly as we waited for Bora
to arrive. 'He's coming today and then
tomorrow we're travelling by one of his boats to
interview the government official, to ask why
he's choosing to ignore Bora's evidence that
poachers are using boats to smuggle gibbons
out of Cambodia,' Mum said. 'I wonder if I'll
be allowed to record the interview,' she added,
talking to herself. 'I wish I had someone to take
notes for me . . .'

I remember thinking that it was more
serious than I first realised. I didn't know that
disappearing gibbons meant they were being
poached and smuggled away. I wanted to find
out more and maybe Mum needed an assistant.

'I'll come and help,' I said immediately.

Mum laughed. 'I think this job is a bit big for you. Maybe when you're older.'

I looked away and watched the waves roll over the sand. Her words stung.

I wonder what she'd think if she could see me now. Coconut slayer!

Bora arrived a few minutes later. He was an older man with a round face and a greying beard, wearing a shirt and shorts. A girl was with him. She looked a few years older than me – sixteen perhaps – and was wearing a pink tie-dye top and matching leggings with bright green sandals.

Mum ran up to them clutching her big straw hat and hugged them both.

'This is my dear old friend, Bora,' Mum said to us, with her arm over his shoulders.

Bora smiled happily and greeted us all. We all stood up and Dad shook his hand and Olly waved at them.

'This is my niece, Vanna,' said Bora.

'Hey,' I said.

Vanna nodded at me but didn't smile. Her long dark hair was side parted and swept up in a ponytail with a scrunchie.

'Vanna's been helping drive the boats at the weekend,' said Bora. 'She's the best driver I know.' He sounded proud.

Mum led us over to the table. She seemed to take to Vanna straight away. She asked her questions about living by the sea and what it was like to grow up in Cambodia. Vanna's replies were always one-word answers. I remember thinking it sounded cool to grow up by the sea and how I'd like to become friends with Vanna, if Mum ever gave me a chance.

'When are we going to see the monkeys?' asked Olly as he climbed up to his chair.

'The gibbons we're going to search for are apes actually, not monkeys,' Bora corrected him.

'What's the difference between a monkey and an ape?' I asked, feeling much more interested in it all after meeting Bora and Vanna and learning about the poaching.

'Well, they're two different groups of primates. One of the main physical differences is apes don't have tails and monkeys usually do. The cool thing is that humans are apes too. That means we're very closely related to the gibbons. The gibbons generally get forgotten about by a lot of people because they're small and technically called lesser apes – but they're just as important as orangutans and all the other great apes!'

'How come you know so much about them?' asked Olly.

'The yellow cheeked gibbons live in the northeast of Cambodia where I grew up. Years ago your mum stayed there with us,' Bora had replied.

Mum nodded. 'That was when I was just starting out as a journalist.'

'And before I had my boats,' said Bora. 'Unfortunately, since then many gibbons have been poached for meat or to make medicine, or sold to the pet and tourist trade. That's not to mention them losing their habitat to development.'

'Tell me more about the gibbons,' Mum said eagerly. 'What makes you think they're being poached and smuggled away here?'

'A month ago I was showing some tourists Unicorn Island—'

'Unicorn Island?' Olly interrupted in awe. 'Are there really unicorns there?'

Bora laughed. 'Sadly, no. I just nicknamed it that because it has a pointy rock on top of it.'

Olly looked disappointed, and Dad ruffled his hair while Bora continued. 'I'd stopped the boat to let them take their photographs when I noticed another boat come speeding past. It was going much faster than it should have been, so I looked round, and that's when I saw it had a caged gibbon on board. Even though they were speeding, I managed to take a photograph, see?' Bora passed his phone around. 'It's definitely a gibbon. You can see its golden cheeks and long arms.'

Mum nodded. 'Who have you shown this to?'

'The government official, Mr Sok. He said the image wasn't enough to warrant an investigation. Too blurry.'

Dad leant forward. 'It *is* a little blurry.'

Mum glared at him.

'But I can tell it's a gibbon, like you said,' Dad added hastily.

Bora continued. 'It's not the only evidence. There are other people who have spotted cages being loaded on to boats that Mr Sok could interview. And many people have claimed to hear gibbons howl in the early hours of the morning, even though wild gibbons don't live in this part of Cambodia.' Bora shrugged. 'I can feel it in my heart that something's not right.'

Mum nodded solemnly.

'I just want to make sure the gibbons are safe,' said Bora. 'That they survive and don't disappear. I want Vanna and my daughter and son to be able to know them. They're special to our country.'

Losing the gibbons in Cambodia would be like if a badger or hedgehog went extinct back home, I had thought.

'Do you think Mr Sok will listen to me?' asked Mum.

'You're an international journalist. I'm hoping the world will listen to you,' Bora replied.

Mum smiled. 'One way or another, we'll make sure they hear your story.'

Bora placed a hand on her shoulder. 'I'm so happy you're all here. Come, let's take a photo to celebrate.'

He ushered us all in to a selfie, with our faces squeezed into the frame, my head next to Vanna's and Olly's. I smiled and Olly stuck his tongue out.

'Can I come with you tomorrow to meet Mr Sok?' I asked.

'We have to leave early, just as it gets light. It's a long journey to the city Mr Sok lives in. We'll be gone before you're even awake,' Mum said, stroking my hair.

'So when are *we* going to see the gibbons?' I asked.

'Next week,' said Mum. 'We're going to travel together to the northeast and see if we can spot any there. I want to interview local people to see if they've noticed any gibbons disappearing.'

I turned to Vanna. 'Are you staying with us tomorrow while they go and investigate?' I asked, hoping that we could hang out.

'I'm driving the boat,' said Vanna.

'Wait, Vanna's going?' I asked Mum. 'Why can't I come too?'

'I'm sorry darling,' said Mum. 'You're not old enough to come with me this time. Stay here with Olly and Dad. You'll have fun and I'll tell you all about it when I get back.'

Vanna smiled sympathetically at me which took me by surprise – it was the first time I'd noticed her smile – but even then I couldn't bring myself to smile back.

If only I'd listened to Mum. I wouldn't be here right now.

later afternoon

As I was writing, I suddenly felt dizzy, but I went for a dip in the ocean and I'm feeling better now. The water was cool and calm. Seaweed swayed around my feet. I lay on my back and floated on the surface until memories of the shipwreck and Vanna screaming flooded back and I had to get out.

I can't get Vanna out of my mind today. In a way, it's sort of her fault I'm here – it was because of her that I decided to sneak on to the boat. I didn't want to be left behind like a little kid while she got to go with my mum. I keep wondering where she is now. If she's somewhere on this island or lost at sea ... or worse.

I didn't tell Dad or Olly I was going. I left them a note on my pillow. I wore a long dress over my shorts and T-shirt so I looked smart enough to be in an interview, and packed my notebook in a waterproof bag, in case Mum needed me to write notes for her, along with a pen and a bottle of water. I thought once Mum realised I was on the boat she would realise I'm not a little kid and let me help with the interview. I remember hoping that Dad wouldn't be too worried about me and that Olly wouldn't miss me too much. I was sure he'd enjoy building sandcastles and would barely notice . . .

WAIT – I can hear something!

Evening

Well that's it. I've just missed what was probably my only chance to get off this island.

As I was writing my last entry, I heard a sound in the sky – like an aeroplane or helicopter. It took a second for my brain to register what that meant but as soon as it did, I was running with all my strength, leaping over driftwood and sand dunes along the beach.

It *was* a helicopter – I could see it in the distance and could feel my heart pounding in my chest. I threw my arms up into the air and waved them above my head.

'Help!' I screamed. 'I'm here!'

The helicopter flew straight past the island.

I was sure it had come to rescue me and would circle back any second.

I jumped up and down. I grabbed bits of washed-up rubbish and flung it into the air, hoping to catch the attention of the helicopter one way or another.

I ran along the beach waving my arms with my heart thudding loudly.

But the helicopter showed no sign of turning towards me. It was still facing the wrong direction, heading away from the island. Even as I shouted and screamed, I knew that it was too far away to spot me and would never hear me over the sound of its own blades. I kicked at the sand, furious at the unfairness of it all.

'No,' I whispered.

What if that was my one chance?

The helicopter disappeared over the horizon.

I sank to my knees at the edge of ocean, hit by the possibility that there was no one else coming.

I might never get off this island.

I walked slowly back to my spot in the shade of the trees.

Now I'm thinking of all the things I'll miss if I'm stuck here for ever, all the places that I wanted to go to. Mainly I keep thinking about Mum, Dad and Olly and how I would do anything to hug them and hear them laugh.

I feel as if I've disappeared. And I have no way of coming back.

I can't stop the tears from coming now. A

sob builds up through my body and bursts shaking through my mouth. Another comes and another, until tears are streaming down my face.

I'm crying for Mum and Dad and Olly but also for Vanna. Whatever happened, we were on that boat together and now I have no idea where she is.

I cry until I have no tears left and the tide goes out and the sand turns powdery in the sun.

Then something special happens.

Goldie timidly approaches me from the jungle. She climbs on to my back and wraps her long arms around my neck. I reach up and hold her hand. The warmth of her body feels like a hug and I can't help but smile. I feel a little spark inside me, the same one that makes me get back up and practise a tumble in gymnastics after I've fallen down. It's barely there, just a glimmer, but it *is* there, and it's a feeling I know, a feeling I can work with. In the topsy-turvyness of this all, it's something that I recognise. With the gibbon clinging on to my back, I rise up.

I stand, glaring at the empty sky and clench my fists. I'm not going to let that happen again. The next time a helicopter comes over, I'll be ready. Because before it gets dark I'm going to build something that *won't* be missed from the sky.

Nightfall

Something changed today. I don't know exactly how but I feel different now. Permanently. Like I won't be able to go back to how I was before, before this happened. I don't even remember what it was like to feel like the old me. All I know is that I can't sit around waiting to be rescued any more. I need to survive.

I spent the rest of the day gathering all the rocks that I could, placing them on the beach to spell out the words HELP in giant letters. Then I realised the person flying overhead might not speak English. I didn't know how to write 'help' in Cambodian. I gathered everything up and turned it into a giant X on the sand instead.

I made a flag with a thick stick and the red rag, sticking it deep in the sand, and stood back to admire my work. Next time a helicopter comes – if someone does come again – they won't miss me.

Tomorrow I need to find drinking water and food. Now that I can open them, I've been drinking coconut water and eating coconut flesh but that's not enough, because my stomach feels like it's eating itself and I'm still so thirsty I can hardly think through the brain fog. I'll run out of coconuts soon too.

I only have seven left. There must be something else on this island that people can eat, surely.

DAY 3

Food supplies:

Seven coconuts

To do today:

1. Reach the other side of the island to FIND WATER and FOOD and get rescued
2. Make a fire

Sunrise

I'm having to bat mosquitoes away from my face as I write this. It's sunrise and the sky is streaked with oranges and pinks and the air is filled with the chatter of birds. All night, I'd drifted in and out of sleep, slipping through nightmares about drowning. I finally woke to

Goldie's singing again so I opened my mouth and whistled along, our notes joining the dawn chorus. My tune was a melody of four notes over and over again, sometimes changing key. The moment I joined in she jumped up and down on the branch above me excitedly.

Last night I was hot and covered in sweat and sticky sand when I finished making my X on the beach. So even though it was dark, I went to the water's edge and dipped my toes in and splashed water over my body to wash everything away. As I moved my foot through the sea, the water glistened and shimmered green and blue, like the stars above. I blinked my eyes shut then opened them again. I thought maybe the starvation was affecting my sight. I crouched and ran my hands through the water and it sparkled.

Then I remembered learning about phosphorescence after seeing it on a nature documentary. Sometimes there was algae in the water that glowed. I smiled and pointed my toe and swooshed it around in the warm sea, watching the explosion of glittery light. I could have stared at it for hours, all night long. Little flashes of light in the deep darkness of the ocean. The more I stared at it, the more I believed that maybe, just maybe, I could be OK.

But then suddenly I was crying again.

Truth is, I was absolutely terrified. I still am. I want to get off this island. I'm getting weaker every day. But I know that Mum and Dad will never stop searching until they find me and that eventually they'll find out where I am. I just have to stay alive long enough for that to happen. I have to find a way to survive on this island, like the gibbon.

Last night my heart was racing as I walked back through the jungle in the darkness. It's a different kind of darkness here to the one that I'm used to. Thick and never-ending. I'd do anything for a torch. Or a street light. I hummed to myself loudly, trying to block out the sound of my fast breaths, my fear. I didn't want any predators to notice it.

I couldn't find Goldie at first and my heart thumped louder and louder. But then I spotted her in a new tree, a few over from the one we had slept in the night before, snoozing upright, high up in a fork in the branches. I called to her and she woke and watched me quizzically.

'I'm going to our tree,' I called to her and she yawned and stretched and followed me. I still felt terrified as I climbed the branches, scanning for snakes, but once I was curled up in my nest with Goldie, the rope I found earlier fastened around my waist and around the trunk of the tree so I wouldn't fall out, I felt better.

Things don't seem nearly as scary this

morning in the sunshine. The rising sun reflects across the sea in a line of shimmery orange towards me.

I'm strangely looking forward to seeing the phosphorescence tonight. I guess it's nice to have something familiar – even if it's only familiar from last night. It's weird the little things that you miss being stranded on an island. I miss the smell of coffee – even though I don't drink it. Mum brews it every day like clockwork. I miss the way Olly gives me a different one of his stuffed toys to cuddle every night. I miss Dad reading to me before bed, even though I'm definitely old enough to read to myself.

That's made me remember something that happened the night before we left for Cambodia, something it might be important for you to know.

61

Dad hadn't come to my room to ask if I wanted to read a chapter of the book we were in the middle of, so I went downstairs to find him. I heard him and Mum arguing in loud whispers in the kitchen. I froze outside the door and listened.

'That happened in South America,' Mum was saying. 'It's a whole different continent.'

'It's happening all over the world,' said Dad. 'And you know it.'

'Yes, and they're not going to get away with it. They're not going to stop us, or to scare us into not doing anything,' Mum replied. 'We need to do the right thing here.'

There was a pause.

'Are you sure it's safe?' asked Dad, his voice softening. 'Just promise me it's safe.'

'It's safe. I'm going to be with an old friend. And you'll be just down the road,' said Mum, gently.

'Are we not going to Cambodia any more?' I asked, pushing the kitchen door open. They were hugging by the kitchen sink.

'No, we're still going,' said Mum, dropping her arms and putting the newspaper in her hands in the recycling bin.

'We might not be,' said Dad, glancing at the recycling bin.

'We most certainly are,' said Mum. 'Have you finished packing?'

I nodded.

'I'll bring your backpack downstairs,' said Dad.

'I'll arrange a taxi for the morning,' said Mum. 'Time for bed, sweetheart.'

Mum squeezed me goodnight as she passed and then they left me standing alone in the kitchen, wondering what on earth that had been about. I waited until they were out of sight and reached in to the bin to pull out the newspaper Mum had placed there. I scanned the front page: something boring about the prime minister; strong winds forecast for the weekend; journalist murdered.

My heart skipped.

I turned to the page the story was on. In Columbia, an environmental journalist had been killed for reporting on trees being cut down illegally. No wonder Dad was worried. Mum is an environmental journalist too.

Dad, if you're reading this. You were right to be concerned.

Morning

As well as going to the other side of the island, I'm going to try and start a fire today. I want to do that for two reasons. The first is that it could be my way off the island. Someone could see it from the ocean and come rescue me. Or Vanna might see, if she's somewhere on this island, lost and scared like me.

And the second reason is that if I have a fire then I can cook fish. I mean, I'd also need something to catch the fish with, but I'll worry about that later.

Goldie is squeaking and playing in the trees above me, climbing higher than I've ever seen her go. I don't know what I'd do without Goldie. She's my only companion on this island – apart from this notebook.

Thank goodness this notebook survived the tossing waves because I don't know what I'd do without it either. It's someone to talk to, here on this island where there are no other people. It helps me set out goals for the day. And it helps me try to make sense of what happened to me.

I'm still hoping by writing everything down, I'll be able to figure out why those people on the other boat were trying to kill me, maybe even who they were.

The thing is, I remember everything that happened but I don't know *why* it happened. Except . . . I think it has something to do with Mum.

Morning, thirty-ish minutes later

On TV they always make starting a fire look easy, like you just rub two sticks together really fast and then you get smoke and, a minute later, a spark. Well, it turns out TV was wrong.

I collected wood and kindling and even shredded the husky bit of the coconut shell, which I thought looked very flammable. I started by trying to rub a stick against a piece of wood. I did it for what felt like hours. Nothing. Next I tried rubbing two sticks together. Still nothing. No spark. No smoke. Nothing.

They really shouldn't make it look so easy on TV. It's not fair to those people who actually get stuck on an island.

Now I'm having a break, sitting in the shade and wiping the sweat from my face. I've eaten a coconut. I don't think I'll *ever* be able to eat enough coconut to feel full though – even if I savour each bite and drip of moisture. My stomach is cramping. I know I need to eat something else – but what?

Midday

I haven't started my journey to the other side of the island yet. It's too hot. I'm going to have to wait until it cools down a bit. I'm sitting and staring at the washed-up litter in front of me.

I've got a new worry about sending this notebook in a bottle out over the waves. There are so many plastic bottles in the ocean – how on earth would anyone spot mine out of the hundreds – no, thousands? It would just get lost, I'm sure. The notebook inside would be mistaken as a food label or more litter. What's even the point?

Amongst the rubbish, I spot a huge empty clam shell. I pick it up – it's the biggest I've ever seen. I didn't know clams got this big. It must be ten times the size of my hand. On the outside are wavy shapes and rough white and grey patterns. The inside is smooth and cool. I've added it to my pile of items. I'm not sure what I could use it for but you never know.

I also found:

- Thirteen plastic bottles
- A toothpick
- A piece of driftwood that looks a bit like a bone

No more fallen coconuts though. I think I've eaten almost all the fallen coconuts on this side of the island.

Midday-ish

I've just followed Goldie through the forest to see if she has a water source. I've been thinking she *must*, otherwise she'd be struggling as much as I am. Plus I love watching her swing gracefully from branch to branch. She has a small round head and a short body. Her arms are longer than her legs. Can you imagine if humans were like that? I bet I'd be extra brilliant at acrobatics.

After several minutes Goldie stopped at a fallen trunk. There was a pool of water in a dip on the top of the trunk. I saw the reflection glistening in the puddle and leapt towards it excitedly. My heart sank as I got closer though

– the water was covered in leaves and flies buzzed across it. It also smelled a bit. Even though I *really* wanted to drink it, I'd learnt my lesson from drinking the sea water. I couldn't risk this puddle water making me sick and losing the small amounts of nutrients I'd managed to get from the coconuts. I sighed and left it for Goldie, who was hanging upside down and happily slurping it up from her hands. At least she has water.

I'm back at the beach, worrying about food and water again. I'm down to three coconuts. I touch my legs. Deep scratches run down them from climbing over the rocks. I rub them and wince. They still feel red and sore. In fact, my skin everywhere feels tight and raw. My nose and shoulders are burnt and peeling. The stinging feeling merges in with the rest of the pain my body is in. If I stop and think about it, I realise that it hurts pretty much everywhere. I can't let it get any worse. I wish I had sun cream.

I've just tried to make sun cream out of mud and sea water, making a kind of paste and smoothing it on to my arms. I remember watching rhinos roll in mud for protection on a nature documentary I saw with Mum. I'll let you know if it works.

Early afternoon

I've given up on making a fire for now. Instead, I'm going to venture into the jungle to see if I can make it across the island. The thought of more coconut is making me feel sick but I'm also still hungry so it's a strange feeling. I should have explored when I had more energy – as soon as I arrived. But I didn't think I would be stuck here for days then. My energy is slipping away. It's getting harder and harder to do anything, even search for food. Which means I'll get weaker. It's a circle that goes round and round. Never stopping. I don't know how it's going to end. Either I get rescued or . . . I don't know.

All I can think about is food. It's been three days since I've eaten anything but coconut. I would do anything for an ice cream or a jam sandwich. Or even a bowl of broccoli (I hate broccoli).

I just ate two coconuts. Now I'm down to one.

I'm going to the other side of the island.

Wish me luck.

Early evening

I'm back at my beach. My trip wasn't a total success but I'm trying my hardest to look at the positives.

Let me explain what happened.

I set off, with Goldie following in the trees above me, swinging with her long arms from branch to branch. I'd fastened the T-shirt on my head and found a big stick to knock through the undergrowth.

'Vanna!' I shouted as I walked. 'Hello!' Maybe she was out here too, hiding in the jungle, wondering where I was.

I stepped over long lines of giant ants. I used my stick to beat down the bushes in my way. I called Vanna's name again.

Goldie stayed in the trees above me the whole way, until one time I looked up and she wasn't there. I panicked. I whistled our song from the morning, hoping to track her down.

She called back to me. I followed the sound, stopping to reply to her and listen to her song until we were both whooping through the forest. At last I spotted her, balancing on a branch, eating some fruit.

I've never moved so quickly, my mouth already watering at the sight of something to eat.

'You found food!' I said and rushed towards her. The fruit was growing in a cluster from the side of a tree trunk. I smelled the fruit to try and figure out what it was. I'd never seen anything like it. It was bulbous and deep purple and about the size of my fist. I had no idea what it was. But as long as it wasn't poisonous, I didn't care. It was food. And I needed food.

I only paused for a second to consider if I should eat it. I decided if Goldie was eating it then it was probably safe for me to eat too, right? Bora had said humans and gibbons were close relatives after all. I raised the fruit to my mouth and touched it with my tongue. It tasted sweet and bitter at the same time. I felt like I almost recognised the taste but I couldn't quite place it. I didn't care. I tore off bite after bite. It was the most delicious thing I'd ever eaten, maybe just because it wasn't coconut. With each mouthful, I could feel my brain clearing, my body re-energising. I ate as many as I could and then picked loads more, unwrapping the T-shirt from my head and turning it into a bag by tying one end together.

I tried to figure out where the tree was in relation to my beach, but I wasn't exactly sure where I was. I'd been walking for hours under the beating sun. I figured I must have almost made it to the other side of the island. It didn't look that big.

I decided to keep walking to try and reach the other side. Everything felt possible again after eating the fruit.

Ahead of me, the forest turned into mangrove swamps which Goldie refused to go near. The water smelled stagnant. I bent over it. It was green and foamy with bugs flying across it. I sighed. I couldn't drink it.

I kept walking, veering around the swamp until I heard the whoosh of the waves. I must have made it to the other side. I picked up my pace, excited to see what was on the other side of the island.

As I clambered down to the beach, though, something didn't look right.

Or rather, something looked familiar.

I'd been here before. But I couldn't have.

I let the fruit thud on to the sand.

I was back at *my* beach. The same beach I started off from.

How was that even possible? I had been sure that I was walking in a straight line.

I sat down and hugged my knees, feeling dizzy again.

That's where I am now, trying to think about the positives. I found the fruit and that's something, right? My stomach is bubbling and growling so I'm waiting to see what happens, but if it doesn't make me sick then I've found food! Well, Goldie found it, I guess.

Goldie has climbed on to my back and is sitting on my neck, tugging at a lock of my hair. She's squeaking at me in the way she does when she wants me to follow her. I've just told her that I'm sorry, I don't have any energy left.

She's not giving up. Now she's singing to me. I'd better see what she wants.

An hour-ish later

I heaved myself up and slowly followed Goldie back into the jungle, focusing on carefully putting one foot in front of the other as she leapt above me on the branches, singing as she went. After a while her singing stopped, and I looked up.

She was hanging upside down from the low branch, almost at the ground. Below her was a rocky area and in the dents of one of the rocks was a large puddle. It looked cleaner than the tree trunk puddle. I could see right through to the rock below and there were no flies in it. As I watched, Goldie reached down with her long arm, dipped her hand into the puddle, and drank from it.

When had it last rained? How long had that water been there? I didn't care. I had to take the risk. I copied the gibbon, scooping the water with my hands into my mouth. It tasted a bit muddy, but it was also the most thirst-quenching liquid I'd ever tasted. I had to stop myself from drinking it all, letting Goldie have another go.

With each sip, I reminded myself that I *am* surviving. I can do it. I have to. I had found food and I had found water. As long as I have those, I can survive here until someone comes to save me.

The fruit reminds me of figs, I realise.

With my belly full of food and water and Goldie clinging to my back in a gibbon hug, I feel the happiest I've felt since I arrived on this island. As bad as things felt earlier, now they feel the opposite. Surviving on this island is a rollercoaster. But you have to celebrate every win otherwise what's the point, right?

I find myself laughing and, above me, Goldie laughs too.

Dusk

It's getting dark and I'm sitting with my toes in the sea, waiting for the phosphorescence to appear. I can already see the first shimmers. The island is a magical place. I wish I had my family or friends here to share it with. If it weren't for the fact that I'm lost and hungry and thirsty, it would be pretty cool.

DAY 4

Food supplies:

- One coconut
- An armful of fig fruit
- Muddy puddle water

To do today:

1. Reach the other side of the island - for real this time!
2. Find more WATER and FOOD

Early morning

Today is exceptionally hot already and I spent the morning lying in the shade with my arms and legs splayed out, like a starfish, exhausted and unable to move. I feel like an egg frying.

I hardly slept. Flashes of the sinking boat kept jolting me from my sleep. Goldie is chattering away above me. She was unimpressed with the mud sun cream concoction I made and tried to groom me earlier, picking out bits of mud from my hair. At one point there was a slight breeze and I almost cried. I'd never been so thankful for a puff of air. I keep thinking about going swimming to cool down, but that means crossing the beach with its scorching sand and glaring sun.

I read once about a shipping container carrying crisps that sank, and all the packets were washed up on beaches, perfectly intact and safe to eat. I dreamt about it last night and now I can't get it out of my head. Imagine a beach full of crisps. I'd settle for a nice packet of chocolate biscuits though. Anything really. I'm down to my last coconut and I pretty much drank all of the puddle yesterday.

Think, Lark. Think.

There must be another way.

Morning

I dragged myself out on to the scorching beach and began to search through the rubbish. There was hardly anything, certainly no crisps or biscuits or magical machine that removes salt from sea water to make it drinkable.

When I first arrived here, I thought my enemy was the snakes or the high ocean waves but really it's the sun. I spend all day hiding from its sharp rays. My whole life right now revolves around what position the sun is in and if there are any clouds to cover it.

I used to dream of summer holidays with my family, of going to the beach and sunbathing. In the cold of winter, I'd imagine lying in the sun. Now I daydream about sinking into a big cold lake. Or stepping out into a snowy winter's day.

Goldie has found a tree to watch me from when I'm on the beach. It's the same branch the toucans use to perch on. The tree with the green coconuts clustered around the top of the trunk is next to it.

Maybe I can find a way to reach them.

Half an hour-ish later

I spent approximately one second considering the best strategy to climb the tall thin trunk – before I ran and jumped on to it. I wrapped my legs and arms around the trunk and shimmied up. I was too thirsty to think about it much. I gripped with my legs and felt the bark graze against my skin. Inch by inch, I got higher and closer to the coconuts. By the time I was halfway up, my leg and arm muscles were burning but I wasn't going to give up then.

Goldie squeaked at me from the next branch.

'Don't worry,' I said. 'I can make it.' I took a deep breath and continued until my head was up in the palm fronds and I could reach up and touch the coconuts. Two bright green and yellow furry caterpillars lay on the leaf next to me.

Goldie squeaked again.

'I know, I know,' I said. 'They look poisonous.' I manoeuvred away from the caterpillars and reached for the coconuts again. I managed to twist one round and round until it broke off and thudded down on to the sand below. I groaned with effort and did the same thing with the next coconut. I repeated the process until I couldn't grip on to the trunk with my legs any more.

I looked down. I had five coconuts lying in

the sand. I must have been ten metres high though, and I still had to shimmy back down. At first I went too quickly and slipped and grated a layer of skin off my palms trying to slow down. I winced. Then, as I was almost at the bottom, another coconut fell and whizzed past my head, narrowly missing me. It would have been enough to kill me, I'm sure. I laughed and shook my head. After all the things that I've survived, imagine if a falling coconut was the thing that got me.

Once I was down, I washed my hands in the sea, letting the salty water clean my palms. They stung but I held them in until all the splinters of bark were out of my skin.

Then I set to work opening one of the coconuts.

It turns out the green coconuts are much easier to open. It's slow going but I can bash them against a rock and peel off the husk before poking the nut inside at the top with a stick to get to the water. The first one I accidentally split in two and the precious water spilled to the ground. I won't make that mistake again. They're filled to the brim with coconut water. Much more thirst quenching than the brown milky ones.

I stood over the pile of coconuts, pleased with myself. There wasn't much flesh in them but the water was perfect. They would keep me going.

Food supplies:

~~Six coconuts~~
~~Five coconuts~~
Four coconuts (I've just opened another one)

Goldie's swinging around the branches above me, stopping to scratch her head and armpit every now and again.

'Let's go to the other side of the island,' I call up to her. 'We'll make it this time. Maybe we'll find Vanna. And if not, maybe it will be a coconut paradise!'

Afternoon

I think we're about halfway through the jungle. Maybe. To be honest, I don't really know, but I'm hoping we are. It's dark and shady under the thick cover of trees. Only a few shafts of light make it all the way to the ground. I can't hear the ocean any more, only the rustle of leaves and birds above. I'm determined we don't walk in circles again this time. I came up with a plan earlier.

Before we left, I washed in the sea. I licked my dry chapped lips with my tongue and winced as they stung. There was sand stuck in my armpits and the creases of my skin. It chafed

and burned as I moved. I took my clothes off
down to my underwear and washed them and
my body, trying not to itch the spots from the
sandflies, which were already red and raw.

I let my clothes dry in the sun before slipping
them back on. When I looked back at the jungle,
I saw Goldie peeking out at me through the
leaves with her big eyes.

'I'm coming,' I said to her.

As I stepped out of the water, a fish floated
next to me. I grabbed its tail and lifted it out of
the sea. Its eyes bulged. I flinched at its rotten
smell and flung it back in to the waves. It had
been dead a while.

I shook my body off and stopped to pick up
an armful of broken fishing net from my pile
of things.

Goldie tilted her head to the side quizzically.

'We can use this to mark the trees that we've
already walked passed so we don't get lost again.

On the way back we can collect more fruit in it,'
I explained to her. 'We can finish what we
collected yesterday now.' I held up a piece of
fruit to her. 'Come and eat.'

She made short bursts of sounds at me and I
realised she wanted me to bring the fruit higher,
into the safety of the trees. I climbed up and we
ate our breakfast in the treetops, surrounded
by chattering birds.

'You coming with me?' I asked, as I climbed
down.

She ran along a branch ahead of me with
her arms in the air, then crouched and jumped
from two feet and caught a branch in the air.

'Hang on,' I said, laughing. 'Wait for me!'

As I battered my way through the thick
jungle, Goldie swung through the trees above
me. It's amazing how fast she is. I stopped and
wiped the sweat off my brow and marked a tree
with the netting. My face felt already like it was

on fire from the heat.

Above me, trees shook and twigs snapped and for a split second I thought it was a whole group of gibbons moving through the branches, but they were small brown monkeys with long tails. I think they're called macaques.

Goldie swung through the trees at top speed into the safety of my arms. I smiled at her. 'Don't worry, they're going now,' I whispered.

After they'd left we continued and I reached an even denser part of the jungle, filled with wide vines blocking every path and thick foliage. I needed something to chop it down; there was no way that I'd make it through with just with my hands. I sighed and sat down, leaning against a broad trunk. A centipede with red legs scuttled over my feet. It was the furthest I'd made it through the jungle. At least it was progress.

I looked up, expecting to see Goldie but the

branches were empty. I sang our song and she answered from further along.

'I can't keep going,' I shouted at her, wishing she would come back.

Goldie reappeared, and poked her head out of the leaves. She squealed excitedly, then dangled upside down beside me, over a mound of earth. She reached down and poked the top of the mound. Red bugs streamed out of the hole and on to her. I shrieked and jumped out of their way.

They must be termites.

Goldie quickly licked the giant red termites off her hand and swallowed them. She lifted her hand to me, offering me some and I shook my head.

'Aren't they stinging you?' I asked, but she wolfed them down.

I've never eaten insects before. I hardly ever even ate meat. Were termites edible for humans? Olly went through a stage of putting everything in his mouth when he was two. I remember Mum telling Dad that he shouldn't let him anywhere near slugs and snails but if he ate an ant it wouldn't be too bad. Termites are sorta like ants, right? I even have a vague memory of learning about the queen termite in one of our *Food Around the World* school topics – they're eaten in Indonesia, I think. But the truth was, even if they *were* edible for humans, I really didn't want to eat termites.

Then I remembered driving through the city after first arriving in Cambodia and seeing a street stall selling fried crickets. I've seen crickets here, jumping all over the island.

Oh God, please let someone rescue me before I have to find a way to catch and cook crickets. I wouldn't know where to begin.

After Goldie had eaten enough, she climbed up on to the branch ahead of me, then chittered.

She swung back and forth, looking at me.

I watched her for a second, trying to figure out what she wanted. Then I understood.

'I'll give it a go,' I said.

I jumped so I could grab on to the branch just below Goldie, then pulled myself up. I stood, balancing, feet on the branch below, holding on to the branch above. Then I began to laugh.

There was a clear path at this height, above the dense foliage below. I just had to reach the next branch. I held on with my arms, as if I was doing the monkey bars, and swung until I could propel myself forward on to the next branch, grasping it and pulling my body across.

I could do this, I thought. All that gymnastics training was paying off!

Goldie screeched with happiness when I showed her what I could do with my acrobatics. She began swinging through the trees ahead of me.

'There's no way I can go as fast as you,' I called.

Up here there were different types of leaves to push past, big ones, green ones, spiky ones, long ones.

It was lighter now that I was closer to the canopy and the blue sky above it. I enjoyed being in the trees, finding ways to move and swing from one to another – until I almost landed on a snake eating a gecko, the wriggling tail still sticking out of its mouth. The tail was blue with red spots.

I opened my own mouth in horror, then closed it again quickly and kept a wide birth. Huge spider webs with giant yellow spiders in the middle of them also dotted my path up in the canopy. One web got stuck in my hair and I almost let go of the branch and fell.

I'm taking a break now, sitting on a branch that's thick enough to hold my weight. Sweat's dripping from my forehead. I'm so thirsty. There has to be some water on the other side. A stream or something. A big puddle. There just *has* to be. I don't know how I'm going to make it back to our tree and my beach, if there's not. At home before I practise I have a snack like a banana and a jam sandwich. Something to give me energy. My body needs fuel. Without it I can't function. I almost slipped and fell three times on the way here. I'm not used to my body letting me down like this.

Goldie is taking a nap. It's hot for her too. I keep forgetting that she's still a little baby. Or a toddler perhaps.

I think about my little brother Olly. He's only a tiny bit bigger than a toddler. I didn't even tell Olly that I was going when I left that morning. I never got to say goodbye to him. I wonder what Dad has told him and where he thinks I am? I hope that Mum is back with them. How much can a four-year-old understand about someone being lost? Where will he think I've been when I get back? Or rather, *if* I get back.

No, I'm not going to think like that.

Time to keep going. Goldie's awake. She's hungry.

later in the afternoon

I started writing in this notebook because I knew that I had to tell someone what had happened to me and how I got here. I hoped maybe someone would find it and I could be rescued. But the longer I'm here, the more I *need* to write everything down. It helps me realise that this is all real.

When I'm lying on the sand, staring up at the bright sky, I can't believe that this is happening to me – but my notebook tells me that it is.

Somehow this notebook makes me feel less alone. When I feel like giving up, I re-read these pages and remind myself that I've got this far. I can keep going. I can do it.

That's what I'm doing now. Because all I really want to do right now is lie down in the sand and give up.

In case you were wondering, I made it to the other side of the island. I'm going to call it Lizard Beach because it's shaped a bit like a lizard's body. But there's no sign of fresh water here. In fact, it's pretty much identical to the beach on my side.

I searched the jungle for food or water. Shouted for Vanna. Nothing. There was nothing in the distance either. No other land. No boats even.

I had really thought that getting to this side of the island might solve all my problems. I was wrong.

So I decided to get what I could from Lizard Beach. Then it wouldn't be a completely wasted trip. The beach was beautiful but it was also covered in litter. I found a flip flop so now I have one plastic bag shoe and one flip flop.

I also gathered:

- Polystyrene bits
- An old shoulder bag to carry the fruit
- More fishing line and a tangled fishing net
- More plastic bottles
- Some string

As I was kicking the sand along the shoreline, I found something else half-buried in the sand. Something purple covered in seaweed. I yanked it up. It was a plastic lilo, still partially inflated.

'Not bad,' I said to Goldie, trying to stay optimistic. 'Not bad at all. This could be a bed!'

Though then I realised I'd have to carry it back to the other side of the island.

In a minute I'm going to take another walk along the beach to make sure I haven't missed anything useful. But I need a bit more time resting in the shade. Part of me is scared I won't make it back to my beach. My legs already feel like they're buckling under my own weight when I walk. Perhaps I'll have to crawl. Goldie is resting too, taking another nap in a tree. She probably needs water too. I offered her some of my coconut water but she didn't drink it.

I miss my family. I want to squeeze Olly and have him nuzzle his head against mine and to be wrapped in the safety of Mum and Dad's arms.

I wonder what Mum, Dad and Olly are doing now? Maybe they're on a boat about to find me. I hope so.

You're probably wondering how I ended up

here all alone in the first place without them. It was my own fault. If I could go back in time and change it, I would.

I think I told you that I'd decided to sneak on to Vanna's boat and go to the interview with Mum. Like I said, I woke up super early, Olly snoring gently on the bed next to me, tiptoed out of bed, and left Dad a note on my pillow.

I remember glancing at the clock in the bedroom when I left and seeing it was exactly four a.m. I wanted to get on the boat before anyone noticed I was missing. My plan was to stow away and surprise Mum once the boat arrived.

After carefully unlocking the door with a quiet click, I tiptoed outside. It was dark and colder than I had expected and I'd wrapped my arms around my body to try and warm myself up. I could hear the waves crashing against the beach. A thick crescent-moon peeked out from the clouds and illuminated the beach below.

I scanned the shoreline for Bora's boat but it wasn't there. It had been here yesterday. I was pretty sure it was red and I was *definitely* sure it had Vanna's name written on the side and there was no boat like that tied up. I knew they couldn't have already left because Mum was still at the hotel.

It was then that something caught my eye out to sea in the distance. I squinted. It was a boat, moving this way. I thought of the gibbon poachers and crouched down behind the outdoor table and chairs to hide in the shadows, watching.

As it got closer I saw the red hull of the boat in the moonlight. Was it Bora's boat? I tried to see the name scrawled across the side but I couldn't make it out.

The boat stopped close to the beach and a girl jumped out. I could see her long hair blowing behind her in the sea breeze. It was Vanna. What was she doing?

Vanna looked around her as if to check if anyone was watching. Then she opened the hatch in the boat deck and looked inside. As the moonlight hit her, I could tell she was still wearing the same clothes as she had been the previous night, a pink tie-dye top and leggings.

I ducked down low as she walked past and went into the hotel. This was my chance. I glanced back to make sure that she was gone, bent low to the ground, and ran across the sand to the boat. I remember how loudly my heart pounded as I waded into the sea, the water noisily splashing against my ankles. I gasped at something touching my feet but it was only seaweed.

I quickly climbed aboard the boat, worried that Vanna could return any minute and spot me. I glanced around at the deck, looking for a place to hide. I spotted the small lifeboat dinghy and scrambled into it. It smelled of rubber and plastic, like a bouncy castle.

And then I waited. Waited for the sun to rise, for Mum, Bora and Vanna to get on the boat, to set off and arrive at their destination.

Afternoon, still, Lizard Beach

I've shaken all the plastic bottles for water and tipped the dregs at the bottom of them into my mouth. They don't taste great, stale and like plastic, but it's something. Goldie wasn't too sure but she did dip her finger in one and lick it.

I also found a broken mirror. I remember learning in school once about how you could use a mirror to bounce the light of the sun a long way – maybe I could use it to signal for help, if another helicopter comes past. I sit by the sea and tilt it this way and that. I have no idea if it works or not. The water's so sparkly out there. It's really just something to do while I sit here and wait until it's cool enough to go back across the island.

It was a mistake to come here during the hottest part of the day. I thought it was later than it was but the sun has stayed high in the sky for hours. When I get back to our beach I'll make a sundial. We made one once in Science and I think I can remember how.

I made a mistake the day I snuck on to Bora's boat too. I forgot a hat. Mum had always been strict about us wearing hats.

I remember how hot it was then too, the boat

swaying beneath me that day, waiting in my hiding place as Mum, Vanna and Bora climbed aboard. I bit my lip to stay silent the whole journey and covered my head with my hands to shade it from the beating sun. I wanted to peek my head up and look out but I stopped myself, thinking how I wanted to surprise Mum when we arrived. Finally, I felt the bump of the boat pulling in to the jetty.

'We're here!' I heard Bora say.

That was my moment.

'Surprise!' I shouted, jumping out from inside the lifeboat. I landed on the deck, next to Mum, Bora and Vanna who all just stared at me.

Usually Mum likes my rule breaking. She always says that I'm finding my own way through the world, that most rules are silly. But that morning she just stood there for ages, swaying.

I looked around at where we were. We were in a bay with other boats and along the shoreline tall buildings rose into the sky.

'What on earth are you doing here?' Mum finally said.

'I thought I could be your assistant?' I offered. I wiped my sweaty forehead and used my hand to shelter my eyes from the glaring sun.

'Oh sweetheart. I meant it when I said you couldn't come,' Mum said. 'What were you thinking?'

I remember the disappointment in her eyes.

'I was just trying to help,' I said.

'Where's your hat?' she asked.

I shook my head. In the darkness of the night I'd forgotten that I'd need one when the sun came up.

'Here, have mine,' she said and handed me her hat and sunglasses. 'And you're not even wearing a life jacket!' She passed me hers. 'What are we going to do with you?'

I remember the corners of her mouth turning up into a pitying smile. Bora and Vanna both looked at me, bemused, but I could tell they were also feeling sorry for me. I felt embarrassed then. And angry that Mum didn't think I was grown-up enough to come with her.

But now, knowing what happened . . . now I think maybe Mum was just trying to protect me.

The sun's gone behind a cloud. Now's my chance to have another look for water – or at least some more coconuts. I'll be back.

A few minutes later

I found water! FRESH WATER!

I came across a stream trickling down the side of a cliff. As soon as I found it, I pushed my mouth up against the flow and let it run into my mouth. It was cool and fresh and the most amazing thing I'd ever drunk. I don't know where it's coming from though. I tried to climb up the cliff to see but I couldn't grip on to anything. I wish I was like those climbers who can scale sheer walls of rock. That would come in handy right now.

I showed Goldie the water and she perked up and we've both spent ages taking it in turns to slurp it up. I've filled two bottles up as well. Now we're ready to cross the island again. My plan is to gather everything I've collected there, like the green coconuts, and bring them back to Lizard Beach. That way we'll be close to the water source.

late afternoon

There's *no way* we're moving to Lizard Beach.

I almost died. Again.

As I headed back into the jungle, I noticed a bit of the beach to the north I hadn't explored yet – it curved around to the right. 'Let's go and check it out,' I said to Goldie. 'There might be something over there.'

Goldie didn't look impressed.

I tucked the lilo under my arm and shielded my eyes with my other hand as I crossed the beach, leaving footprints in the sand behind me.

As I got closer, my heart leapt.

I could see another island.

I ran up to the water's edge and gazed out into the distance. The island wasn't too far away, to the north of this one. I raced along the beach, closer to the shortest crossing point. The island looked similar to this one, maybe a bit bigger, with hills and a thick covering of trees. The channel of water between the islands was crystal clear and I could see seaweed that looked like grass growing on the seabed. I waded in and tiny shiny fish swam in and out of the seagrass by my feet. I even spotted a tiny seahorse. To the left stood the open ocean.

I had to see what was on the other island, North Island. It wasn't far, I was sure I could swim it.

'I'm going to try getting to that island,' I called to Goldie. 'I'll be right back.'

If only I'd known it wouldn't be that easy.

I paddled in to the water, holding the lilo in front of me. I was a good swimmer and it didn't look that deep – but the ground suddenly dropped off and I had to kick my legs. Memories of the sinking boat came flooding back, of tossing and turning in the waves and the roar in my ears. The current was stronger than it looked and I gripped on to the lilo with all my might.

Goldie screeched from the jungle behind me, watching me through the trees. The same short sharp squeak she'd made when the snake was making its way towards me. An alarm call.

I looked back at her and caught sight of her anxious face, mouth open with worry.

'Just a bit further,' I called to her, gritting my teeth. The island didn't look as close now, through the tossing waves. Then I felt a sudden stinging pain in my legs, as if I'd been bitten by a thousand tiny ants. I yanked them under me and peered into the water below. There were tiny jellyfish floating around me.

Then, just ahead of me, I spotted a *gigantic* jellyfish.

It was white and translucent at the same time. It had a boxy shape and floating inside of it was a dead fish. My heart raced. Its tentacles were long, at least two metres.

I scrambled to turn back. First I pulled myself on to the lilo, but it didn't have enough air in it to support my whole body and caved in the middle. I paddled away, thrashing my arms in a backwards butterfly motion, hoping it might scare the jellyfish away. My legs got tangled in the lilo. Adrenaline shot through my body. I knew instinctively that this was *not* a friendly jellyfish. It was too big and ominous looking. And I was in its territory.

I reached the shore and scrambled backwards to get out of the water. The lilo washed away. There was no way I was risking going back in the water to get it. I lay on the sand, panting and looking up at the sky, the clouds blurring together.

Goldie scampered towards me. She climbed on to my upper arm and held my hand.

'I'm OK,' I said to her. 'Don't worry.'

The crossing would have to wait until another day. Hopefully the jellyfish weren't always there. But there's no way I'm moving to Lizard Beach and its jellyfish-infested waters. How will I wash? No. Time to go back to my beach.

Now I'm filling all the plastic bottles I can find with water from the cliff, and gathering all my things into the shoulder bag I found. It's going to take all my energy to lug everything back through the jungle but I have to do it.

Wish me luck.

DAY 5

Food supplies:

- Four litres of drinking water
- Four coconuts
- A termite mound
- Maybe-Figs

To do today:

1. Collect more water from the stream on Lizard Beach
2. Make a sundial
3. Attempt a fire again

Morning

Every day I wake to the morning chorus of the birds and Goldie's singing. I hate the nights and the memories of the boat sinking that haunt my sleep. It's always a relief when I hear her singing each morning. I'm finally awake. It's finally day. And I've made it through another night.

Goldie's haunting melody echoes over the treetops, across the island. For a second this morning, I thought I heard another gibbon join in. I haven't seen any other gibbons here though. I have seen some macaque monkeys but it seems like the main creatures that live here are snakes. Lots of snakes. So many that I've learnt to stomp the ground as I go through the forest so they feel my vibrations and think that I'm something big and get out of the way.

I'm gathering rocks and a stick to make a sundial today.

Five minutes later

I've found a good straight stick at the edge of the jungle and pushed it deep in the sand so that the sun casts a shadow across the ground from it. Is Cambodia in the northern hemisphere or the southern? I'm pretty sure it's just above the equator, in the northern hemisphere, which would mean than my stick would need to point to the north a bit. I can figure out which way north is, based on where the sun rises each morning.

Then I place a stone at the end of the shadow. Next I think I'm supposed to place a new stone on the shadow every hour. I'd forgotten about that bit. I'll have to guess how long an hour is. But it'll give me something to do.

lunch

For lunch I've eaten five of the maybe-figs and
drunk a litre of water. I've been sipping from
the water bottle throughout the day and I feel
so much better but my stomach still hurts from
hunger. I'm thinking if I can get a fire going I
can catch the crabs that dash across the sand
and barbecue them. Or roast crickets. Or bake
termites.

If only I *could* start a fire. It turns out it's
actually impossible. I'm never going anywhere
without matches ever again, just in case.

I'm off to collect more water now from the
stream on Lizard Beach. See you in a bit (unless
the giant jellyfish gets me!).

Waxing Gibbous Moon, evening

I'm back and I have a sundial! I have no idea how accurate it is but it should help me keep track of the time a bit. I think it'll help me a lot. I can make sure I'm resting during the hottest hours of the day and doing everything I need to do in the mornings and late afternoons when it's cooler.

I keep thinking about Vanna. Whether she's somewhere on the island or maybe on the other one. Whether she's made a camp or if she's been rescued already. Or if . . . no, I won't think about that.

I remember her shocked face that day, when I scrambled out of the lifeboat and surprised her, Bora and Mum.

'How long have you been in there?' she

asked, looking worried.

'Since just before you all came on the boat,' I lied.

'I'd better let Dad know,' said Mum.

'Vanna can take her back,' said Bora kindly. 'We won't need the boat again until tonight. We'll walk the rest of the way now.' He'd glanced at his watch. 'We should go now, otherwise we'll miss our appointment.'

'Do I have to?' Vanna asked.

'Oh, come on, it won't take that long. Why don't you see if you can find some dolphins together?' said Bora.

Vanna sighed.

Mum rang Dad. 'I'm sending her back on the boat now,' she said. 'Vanna's going to take her. They'll be fine together. I trust Vanna.'

I remember how Vanna folded her arms and glared at me suspiciously.

'I know about this morning,' I whispered to

Vanna. 'But don't worry, I won't tell on you.'

She froze, her body suddenly stiff.

'What are you talking about?' she asked.

'I'm just saying that your secret's safe with me,' I said and shrugged. I didn't really know what she'd been doing, all I'd seen was her coming back by herself on the boat and looking into the hold – but I figured that she might like me more if she thought I was keeping a secret for her.

'What is it you want?' she asked.

'Nothing,' I shrugged, trying to act cool.

'I guess I can show you some dolphins,' she said reluctantly.

I wanted to know what she'd really been doing but since I'd pretended to know I couldn't exactly ask her. Plus seeing dolphins did sound amazing so I nodded.

Mum got off the phone and kissed me on the forehead. 'Dad will be waiting for you on the beach.' She addressed Vanna. 'Go straight back after the dolphins, OK?'

They disembarked on to a wooden jetty and waved as Vanna started the boat and we drove out into the ocean. So much for my big plan to help Mum and prove I was grown up.

And that was the last time I saw Mum's face. Waving at me from the jetty. She had the same look on her face as Goldie did when I paddled out on the lilo yesterday. Worried. Anxious.

Goldie has barely left my side since that moment. She's sleeping on the branch next to me right now. Maybe she thought that I wouldn't come back. Maybe she needs me here as much as I need her.

DAY 6

Food supplies:

- Three coconuts
- Two litres of water
- Termite mound

To do today:

1. Search the beach
2. Collect water
3. Collect more fruit

Mid-morning

Mum, Dad, if you're reading this – I have a confession. I haven't brushed my teeth in days. I've scraped off the surface with my nail but they still feel really furry. I didn't think that keeping clean would be a problem on an island surrounded by water but after the jellyfish incident (I've nicknamed her Belladonna) I haven't felt like venturing into the sea. So when you rescue me, just a heads-up, I might be a bit stinky. It's impossible not to sweat loads in the heat and humidity. My hair feels like a giant ball of matted frizz. I've managed to comb through some of it with my fingers.

This morning I also did something I never thought I'd do. I found a washed-up bottle that had some brown liquid in the bottom. It smelled like cola so I tasted a tiny bit and I could tell it was definitely some kind of fizzy drink. An explosion of sweetness in my mouth. It was completely flat but now I'm having tiny little sips and I can already feel the sugar rushing through me. It feels fantastic.

This island really would be paradise if I was just visiting for a day. The sea is emerald-blue.

It's shallow for a while so you can stand in the warm water and watch the fish swimming about below you. Today I saw a stingray. The sand is soft and fine, sometimes pinkish in the sunlight.

I found a broken clam shell along the shoreline that has a razor-sharp edge and I'm going to try and fasten it to a stick to make a knife.

Midday

I'm in the jungle. I used up all my energy making a clam-knife and gathering food, and now I'm having a sugar crash. At least I'm not the only one. Goldie's next to me, reclining against a tree trunk, above the pile of maybe-figs that we've collected.

I've noticed that in the middle of the day when it's really hot Goldie doesn't do much. She looks peaceful with her eyes half closed. The hair on her head is tufted into a crest. At home, I'm always doing something – reading or on the phone to Sophia or practising acrobatics. I hardly spend any time like the gibbon, just being.

I crane my neck trying to see if she's looking at something, but there's nothing there.

A few minutes later

I wanted to carry the maybe-figs back to the beach, but I decided to try and be like Goldie, just for a bit, so I copied her and stayed very still. I felt the faint breeze against my cheeks and watched the ground below, teeming with ants and bugs and leaves moving. At first I felt restless, desperate to keep working through my survival list. Here on the island, surviving means doing one thing after another and I always feel more and more anxious as the day gets on and the sun gets higher in the sky. It feels like a race against time to get everything done before nightfall. But after a while of copying Goldie, I felt a stillness. Then I realised. Maybe Goldie was telling me to stop and rest.

Trouble is, I can only stay still for a few seconds. Recently, whenever I'm not doing something, memories of what happened on the boat keep coming flooding back to me, filling my body with terror again. I can't shake them. I keep waking up in the middle of the night dripping in cold sweat.

When I was little and I had a nightmare Mum always told me to write it down and then we'd catch the nightmare and trap it in a locked box. I had the key to my own box of nightmares.

Maybe I can trap the nightmare of what happened in this notebook, even if I don't have a locked box to put it in after. It's worth a try.

Here goes . . .

After an hour of travelling with Vanna, I was beginning to think that she had lied about being able to show me dolphins, when she slowed the boat.

'The dolphins are usually around here,' she said. 'It's one of their favourite places.'

I leant over the side of the boat and gazed down into the deep dark waters.

I saw the ripple of water and the grey shape of a creature underneath. A nose and then . . . a dolphin body arched out of the waves, jumping. Foaming spray flew into the air.

'There!' I shouted. I spotted another one. 'And over there!' Suddenly dolphins were all around us, squeaking and splashing. I wanted to lean over the side of the boat to see them close up, but the life jacket was too big and bulky. I removed it to get a better look.

I was so fixated on the dolphins that I didn't

see the boat coming up behind us.

I didn't hear the thrum of the engine picking up speed.

If I had, maybe we would have had more time to prepare, more time to brace. Perhaps Vanna could have got us away.

If only we'd noticed the boat heading straight for us.

I didn't realise until it was too late. Until the boat, much bigger than ours, came crashing into us.

Afternoon lunch

Goldie has brought me a spider to share with her.

I tried to tell her that I don't want it but she looked so pleased with herself and excited that I've just pretended to eat a furry leg. I hope she doesn't bring me more.

I'm grateful for a break from reliving the boat crash and a few minutes to remember that I'm here with Goldie and I'm alive, somehow. I'm sipping some of my water and eating a few maybe-figs. But now that I've started, I need to keep writing. It feels important, like it's the key to figuring all of this mess out.

When I close my eyes I can see Vanna, standing next to me on the deck in the moment of the crash. My ears ring from the smash of the collision. I can see the ocean roaring around us, Vanna lying on the deck . . .

'Are you OK?' I shouted.

'I think so. Are you?' she replied as she pulled herself up. She ran to the back of the boat, slipping on the wet deck and screamed at the boat behind us. 'Hey! What do you think you're doing?'

I glanced back. The boat was reversing away from us.

I remember how I thought in that moment that it was over. They were leaving.

If only I'd realised they were about to come back.

'What just happened?' I asked shakily.

Vanna squinted at the boat. 'It's them,' she said under her breath.

I wondered who 'them' was.

The big boat engine stopped, then switched on, louder. Huge waves churned out from behind it. The boat changed direction, heading back towards us.

'Stop!' shouted Vanna and she waved her arms up and down. 'It's me!'

'You know them?' I asked, confused. 'What are they doing?'

The boat continued to head straight towards us. Vanna revved the outboard motor.

Compared to the big boat though, we were chugging forward at a snail's pace.

'They're gaining on us!' I said.

'The gibbon,' said Vanna. 'They don't know I have the gibbon.' Vanna pointed at me to take the steering arm.

I grabbed it with shaky hands and glanced backwards at the boat. It barrelled towards us with its bulky steel hull.

Vanna heaved up a hatch in the deck.

'Help me!' she shouted.

I hesitated, not wanting to leave the boat with no one at the wheel. I glanced around at the items on the deck. A coiled-up rope. A backpack. A five-litre bottle of water. I grabbed the water and heaved it up against the steering arm to keep the boat going forwards.

The top of Vanna's body had disappeared into the hatch. 'Here, take this,' she said.

She was holding a cage. I grabbed the sides to

steady it. Inside was a tiny furry creature. A gibbon. It was the last thing I expected her to give me. A real-life gibbon.

I gasped, shocked. 'Why do you have a gibbon?' I'd asked.

'I can't explain now. Just help me. We need to show them the gibbon. Hold the cage up. I'll open it.'

I lifted the cage up so that Vanna could undo the padlock.

She unlocked it – just as the boat crashed into us again with an enormous bang. The cage went flying out of my hands. I lost my balance as the boat rocked underneath me. I fell. And this time, the deck didn't catch me. I kept falling until I hit water. The cold shocked my body all the way to my bones. Water filled my ears and nostrils. Sound was muted. Panic filled my chest.

I opened my eyes, completely submerged

under the waves. Everything was a shimmering blue. I thrashed my arms and kicked my legs, trying to make it back to the surface against the current, dying to breathe.

My head burst through the surface and suddenly everything was loud and roaring. People shouting. The boat creaking. The gibbon screeching.

Mum's hat bobbed away from me in the current.

Where was the gibbon?

I looked around, treading water, and spotted the boat, just in time to see the cage slide off the deck and into the sea with a splash.

It's hard remembering all this, but it feels important. I glance at Goldie just to remind myself that she's safe now – we survived the crash. She's beautiful, her black hair tufted into a crest on top of her head, her golden cheeks, hairless black face and big eyes watching me. I stroke her head and back. She lifts her shoulders and leans against me.

When the cage slipped into the water, I'd swum after it. Somehow I managed to get to her. I really have no idea how. It was as if there was an invisible force pulling me towards Goldie.

She was clinging on to the top of the cage as it sank, her big eyes wide and scared. When I grabbed the cage, she shrieked and clutched on to the bars. I pulled at the cage door, opened it, and gently clasped her tiny body. All I could do was hold her with one hand above the surface and tread water. The boat that rammed in to us was driving away, speeding off in the other direction.

'Help!' I shouted. 'Vanna?' I searched for signs of her on the boat and in the water but I couldn't see her anywhere.

The current was carrying me further and

further away from our boat. I tried to swim back to it, but with the gibbon it was impossible.

I was all alone. I pictured myself now – a tiny dot in a huge ocean, drifting further and further away from everything.

'Don't go!' I shouted after the distant boat. 'You can't leave us here.'

I remember the feeling of my legs starting to give out. My clothes were heavy, pulling me down. I tried to think – what were you supposed to do when you were tired in the water? Then it came to me. *Float*. I knew I couldn't keep fighting the current so instead I turned on to my back and positioned the gibbon on my chest, letting the water hold me up. And then I just let the current take us. The waves swirled and frothed around and over me, never ending, pulling me this way and that.

Even though I was floating, it still took energy to keep the gibbon above water.

'I'm sorry,' I said to her. 'I don't know how much longer I can keep going.'

A big wave crashed over the top of me.

I was sinking. I remember wondering, *what does it feel like to drown*?

It was then that I felt something brush against me in the sea. The waters below me were deep and dark. I was scared of the creatures that lurked under the waves. I knew there were big fish out there. *Please don't be a shark*, I thought. But I didn't feel teeth. I felt a nudging, like a dog's nose pushing against you when it wants to go on a walk. Then I heard a clicking and squeaking and knew. It was a dolphin. It was a dolphin holding me up, keeping me and the gibbon from drowning.

I want to keep writing. It's a relief to finally get this all out. But the memories are making me tremble. What if I survived and Vanna didn't?

The sundial says it's three p.m. I need to collect water before it gets too late.

I'll be back.

Evening

I'd love to see the dolphin again. To thank it. I don't think I would have survived without its help. Really, when I think about it, I've been so lucky.

I just need one more bit of luck. To get rescued.

I look out into the ocean now on my side of the island but it's still and calm. There's no sign of dolphins or boats. I must really be in the middle of nowhere.

I've just had a thought. What if I've ended up in a Bermuda Triangle type situation? Loads of ships went missing in the Bermuda Triangle and they never found the wreckage. What if something like that's happened to me? What if there's a second Bermuda Triangle no one knows about *here*? That would explain why I haven't been rescued yet, if I'm in some sort of other dimension or something. But then, if that's the case, how do I get out?

If I don't make it off this island, I need to at least leave something behind that explains what happened to me, so that maybe one day someone will find it, and the people responsible for the crash can be found. The problem is, I know *what* happened to me, but I still don't understand *why*. Why did that other boat crash into us on purpose? Who were the people on it? And what does Vanna have to do with it all?

I keep thinking about Mum too. I feel like I've let her down. She's a journalist, she would have figured out the answers to all these questions by now – but I'm still stuck. I've tried to piece everything together, but my thoughts keep turning to food and to drinking water and orange juice, litres and litres of it. The one with the bits in it.

Night

I'm writing this by the light of the moon as I dip my toes in the water and phosphorescence shimmers around me. Now that I've started writing about the crash, I can't stop. I want to get it all out before I go to bed. That way, I may actually be able to sleep for once.

Two years ago, in school, my class completed a water safety certificate and part of it was jumping in the local swimming pool with our clothes on. I remember being surprised at how heavy my clothes instantly became in the water. I never thought for a second that I'd need the training in real life, but that day in the sea, as the dolphin struggled to keep me and the gibbon above water, it came back to me, and I knew what to do. One arm at a time, I wriggled out of my long flowy dress and let it wash off me. It was much easier to say afloat in my shorts and T-shirt.

The dolphin kept pushing me forward, helping me swim, until I felt something solid underneath my feet. It was a huge rock. I collapsed, gasping, on to it. I turned back to the dolphin, only then noticing more of them in the distance.

'Thank you,' I whispered after them. They had just saved my life. Of that I was certain. I hoped that they'd helped Vanna too, wherever she was.

I lay spreadeagled on the rock. It was warm beneath my face. Water lapped around me.

After a few minutes, I felt recovered enough to lift my head and look at my surroundings.

The dolphins had delivered us to an island. I carefully picked up the gibbon and clambered with her over the slippery rocks, past mangroves and green swamps, into the shade of the jungle. I kept a wide berth around the swamp, feeling there were bound to be snakes and creatures in those murky waters.

Through the trees I saw the glisten of white sand.

That's where I need to go. That's where we'll get help.

The first moment that I set eyes on this beach I knew that this was where I would be safe.

So that's how the boat sank, how I got here. The more I think about it, the more I'm convinced the people on the other boat were trying to kill us. They were trying to jolt us overboard and, when they finally managed to do it, they left us in the ocean to die.

Now that I've written it down, I hope the nightmares will stop.

DAY 7

Food supplies:

- Three litres of water (Four litres is how much I can carry at a time from the stream on Lizard Beach, and I've already drunk one whole litre from yesterday's trip!)
- One coconut
- No food (unless you count the termite mound)

To do today:

1. Check the beach for anything useful
2. Figure out why the people on the boat were trying to kill us
3. Collect water
4. Start a fire

Sunrise

Last night I slept well for the first time since landing on this island. I woke up stiff and uncomfortable but I didn't mind that. I had still dreamt of water, but this time I wasn't filled with terror that Goldie and I were about to die. Instead I woke up with questions swimming in my mind.

Why did the other boat target us?

Why did Vanna have the gibbon?

How did Vanna know those people?

It was as if writing down the story of the boat crash had freed up space in my mind to process everything else. I wish I'd done it sooner.

Mornings with Goldie have become my favourite time of day. We sing together and for a few minutes I can forget about everything that's happening and focus on the music filling the sky.

Once it's over, I'm faced with another long, hot day.

Goldie has brought me a present. A piece of fruit that looks a bit like an almond. I've eaten all of the bulbous fig-like fruit already. I quickly discovered that the ones that weren't purple weren't ripe. They were extremely bitter and made all the moisture leave my mouth. Goldie is an expert at finding fruit but some of the things she's brought me – like the spider – I don't want to eat. This almond-shaped fruit tastes nice though.

Mid-morning

I've found an empty tin can on today's morning check of the beach. If only it had baked beans inside it. I'm not ready to eat a spider leg but I do need something else to eat, that's certain. Fruit isn't enough, I'm hungry all the time.

After resting, my body felt a bit stronger and I explored further along the beach, over the rocks, desperate for something to eat. I brought the tin can to collect things in.

Years ago we stayed with one of Mum's friends on the coast in Scotland and she took us on to the rocks to harvest limpets. I searched the rocks here for little shells. There weren't any limpets, but there were snails. I picked one up, turning it over and peering inside. It looked like a slug inside – not very appetising. I wasn't even sure if they were edible, but I collected some of the biggest ones in the tin can, covering them with sea water.

In Scotland we'd collected the limpets in a bucket and cooked them on a fire. That's what I really need here: a fire.

A few minutes later

I made a pile of kindling from a few scrunched up pages from my notebook (I really didn't want to waste any pages but I'm getting desperate) and put it on top of a piece of dry driftwood. Then I stood a straight stick up on top of it and rubbed and rubbed the stick between my hands so that it twisted back and forth, creating friction. My hands were raw and my arm muscles ached but there was nothing. No spark. No smoke. And I was still absolutely ravenous.

I rubbed my eyes, defeated, too exhausted to cry, or be angry. I just sighed. I'd eaten all the coconuts on the ground and I couldn't reach the ones left in the trees. The maybe-fig fruit is gone. I don't know where Goldie got the almond fruit or if there's any more of that. It seems like I've eaten everything I can on this island.

I can't bring myself to eat raw snails.

Another few minutes later

I tipped the snails back out into the sea with the shoals of shimmering fish. A spiky fish swam close to my feet and I darted out of the way. I don't know anything about fish. But I know that spiky fish should be avoided at all costs. Now I'm lying in the sand on my stomach, thinking about the things that I miss. My family. My friends. Laughing together (that's what I miss the most). Food (of course). Music. (There's one song that's been stuck in my head that I can't remember all the lyrics to so I've had to make them up.)

One thing I don't miss is all the extra stuff I did at home. Mum's always getting me to try other things alongside school and acrobatics, like learning Japanese or joining the school magazine. I never want to let her down. But the truth is, I'm exhausted by the time I go to bed and then I lie awake worrying about how much I have to do the next day. The only time I'm not worrying is during acrobatics and that's because if I'm not present then I'll mess up and hurt myself.

Here on the island there's no one to tell me to do anything. Only myself. But sometimes the voice in my head is the worst of all. Even right now, the voice is telling me I should be searching for food, but I'm too tired. And really, I need to rest, just like Goldie showed me. That's important too, right?

I'm watching the sand blow over the beach, creating patterns, drawing in the sand with my finger. I'm going to draw Goldie and me.

Afternoon

When the sun got slightly lower in the sky, and my sundial told me it was four p.m., I decided to walk along the beach again to try and find something washed up that I could eat. I didn't find any food – I found something even better.

I spotted a metal ring glistening in the light and I bent to uncover a pair of glasses in the sand. One of the eye lenses was smashed but the right one was intact. Immediately, I had an idea. In school once we had started a fire with a magnifying glass – maybe I could do the same thing with the lens from the glasses. I quickly washed them in the sea before running over to the kindling pile. I'd saved the ripped-out pages from my notebook and laid them in the full sun and held the glasses up, shining the sunlight through the lens and on to the paper. I could see the light as a dot. I moved the glasses back and forth, making the dot as round and small as possible. Then I held the glasses as still as I could in that position.

'Come on,' I muttered. 'Come on.'

A moment later, there was a puff of smoke. It had worked. It had actually worked! I couldn't believe it. I pulled the kindling on top and watched as it caught, the wood crackling and glowing. I slowly added twigs, then sticks, then some bigger fallen branches I'd found until the fire blazed and sparks flew up in the sky. With each *pop* and spark I wished for someone to see it, for someone to rescue me and the gibbon, for Vanna to be OK.

Half an hour later

As soon as I was sure the fire wasn't going to burn out, I went back and collected some more snails in my tin can. Now I've balanced the can on top of two rocks and am boiling the snails in sea water. The tin can is flickering blue and green in the flames.

I'm about to eat my first hot meal on this island. Bon appétit!

Five minutes later

I managed to eat three snails. They're pretty disgusting. But even that can't dampen my mood. Next I'll try boiled termites, or maybe crabs, although neither are very easy to catch.

I watch the thick smoke from the fire rise into the sky with embers. Someone will see it and come. I know they will.

Evening

As the sun set tonight, I did a fire dance – a half-hearted cartwheel in the sand (it was all I had the energy for).

Goldie is watching me, waiting for me to

come to bed in the trees. But I want to stay by the fire and sleep on the ground, completely horizontally for once. I'm fed up of sleeping mainly upright in the tree. It's like having to sleep on an aeroplane chair every night. I don't want to leave Goldie alone though.

I wonder where Goldie came from or where her family are. I wish I could tell her that we'll find her family but I don't know that for sure so I keep quiet and watch the fire instead.

Night

Slowly, I can feel the haze lifting and more details coming back to me about the boat crash. Maybe the haze was my brain's survival mechanism. It forced me to focus on staying alive and nothing else. Maybe the fact that the fogginess in my mind is lifting means that now I am successfully surviving. Or maybe my body is so tired it's given up on survival mode. I'm not sure.

I decide to write down the things that I know are true. It's not very much:

1. Vanna knew that Goldie was stowed away on her boat.
2. She also knew the men who attacked us.

And also:

3. Vanna was hiding something. I'm pretty sure she wasn't supposed to be out by herself driving the boat that morning I spotted her looking in the hatch. What had she been doing?

Now that I think about it, Vanna seemed uneasy around us from the first time we met. Did she know that the men were going to come after

Goldie and so she hid her in the boat? But if she knew we were in danger, why wouldn't she tell her uncle? None of it makes any sense.

DAY 8

Morning

Well, so much for being rescued. Everything feels hopeless again. Why can't the island give me a break?

I'd eventually gone back to our tree last night to keep Goldie company. I'd fallen asleep upright as usual, when I was woken by a strange feeling. I felt the wind first, howling and blustering through the leaves. Then I realised my entire branch was swaying. My eyes snapped open and I gripped on to the trunk of the tree. I thought that I was going to fall out! Thunder boomed overhead. It was about to rain.

The fire.

It took me so long to get this fire going, I couldn't let it go out.

What if a search helicopter came and I missed

it because I let the fire go out?

I checked that Goldie was safe before climbing down and dashing through the trees to the beach. I looked out over the sea. The ocean was angry and huge waves were rising and breaking, each with a loud slap. Purple lightning forked through the dark sky.

I gathered as much wood as I could, throwing it on top of the struggling flames. I lugged three fallen big branches across the beach and tried to make a tepee shelter over the fire but I couldn't get it to stay. I needed another pair of hands. Lightning flashed all around me.

'Help!' I shouted. 'The fire! I have to protect the fire!'

I knew it was useless. There was no one there to help me.

I looked around for anything that I could use to protect the flames from the coming storm.

The palm fronds.

They could be an umbrella.

There were a few dead ones scattered near me so I gathered them. I needed more but I didn't have a knife to cut down the bigger ones still attached to the trees. The dark clouds hung low in the sky overhead.

Then the rain poured from the sky. Huge droplets fell around me. The fire hissed and singed, sending out thick smoke. I held the palm fronds over the flames but the rain was too heavy and was being blown sideways towards the fire by the strong winds.

In less than a minute, the flames were gone. Embers shone orange.

'No,' I said, kneeling next to them. 'You're our only hope of being found and getting off this island. You're my way back to Mum and Dad and Olly.'

The embers were being extinguished by each raindrop.

'Come back,' I said, desperately blowing on them. 'Come back.'

The wind howled and the rain slashed around me. It dripped down my face. I was absolutely drenched. Frogs croaked and screamed in the jungle.

I cried into the rain and kicked at the fire. There was nothing I could do. Everything was too wet to start another fire, plus I needed the sun which was hidden behind the thick clouds and probably would be tomorrow too. If a rescue helicopter came today they'd miss me. And they might not come a third time.

I wish that we'd never come on this trip. I wish that I'd never hidden in the boat to see Mum.

I sank down into the wet sand and shivered and cried, while the storm raged around me.

Mid-morning

It was Goldie who brought me back from the hopelessness of it all. Goldie who sang softly and climbed down to me and hugged me tightly, Goldie who insisted that I retreat back to the trees. Maybe it was because she was scared without me, but I think that it was because she knew that I was sad too.

As I walked back with Goldie, a huge branch fell right in front of us with a crack, and I realised how dangerous this storm was. Even now that we're in the trees, branches are snapping and thudding to the ground around me.

When we got back to our tree, we huddled together. I watched Goldie grooming herself, sucking the water off her fur. And then I realised – WATER! I'd been so worried about the fire that I forgot that the rain could be a water source. I opened my mouth and let the droplets fall in. Then I raced back down to the beach and gathered my plastic bottles and pushed them upright into the sand. It was better than nothing. Maybe they would collect enough water that I wouldn't have to travel back to Lizard Beach again to refill them for a while.

I remembered the huge clam shells that I'd collected and my tin and I laid them out too. The water pooled in them quicker than in the bottles.

Even though I'm happy to have more water, I miss the heat of the sun. I didn't think I'd *ever* want the burning sun back again, but I think being cold and wet is even worse than being hot. It's scary too. A bolt of lightning just flashed across the whole sky, reaching down and hitting the sea.

A bit later

When the morning light finally appeared, grey and stormy, I realised that the rain had washed away all of my help signs – and it's still pouring down. I'm soaking and freezing. My fingers have become all wrinkled, like when you've been in the bath or in the swimming pool for too long. Every time the rain stops for a bit, I wipe them on the tree and then on my clothes but no matter what I do I just can't get dry.

But my clam shell water collection system has worked really well. When there was a lull in the thunder, I climbed down to retrieve them. I lifted one to my lips and let the water pour down my throat and glugged it all back before leaving it to fill up again with rain water. I drank and drank. I feel a bit queasy now but it was worth it.

Midday

I've figured something out. Something pretty big. But the thing that made me realise it was something small. A straw hat.

When the rain finally eased off a bit, Goldie and I climbed down from our tree and peeked out from the jungle. The storm had washed up much more than normal on to the beach so I decided to scour the sand for anything that could be of use. And that's when I saw something that made me stop, heart thudding.

A large section of red coloured wood was floating in and out with the tide. Then I saw the letters *NA* in white on the side and rope and wood planks all tangled up on it.

Our boat.

I raced to the shore, leaving Goldie behind in the jungle. Bora's boat was called *Vanna*. This had to be it. I approached it slowly, scared of what I might find. Images of Vanna falling into the water and getting trapped in the ropes flashed through my mind. I forced myself to look – and my heart leapt as I spotted a bright orange life jacket crumpled in the corner – but there was no Vanna there.

I stuffed the life jacket under my armpit and dragged the boat wreck closer to shore so it wouldn't float away. On the beach I pulled off the tangled rope and rubbed my hands over the letters.

Then I recognised something caught in one of the splintered planks. Mum's white straw hat, all ripped and shredded. I worked it out from the wood, trying not to tear it even further. I hugged it to my chest. A lump swelled in the back of my throat.

I'm so sorry, Mum. If you're reading this, I never meant for any of this to happen. I should have listened to you. I just wanted to spend time with you.

I put the hat on even though it's falling apart, pretending I'm an adult like Mum, an adult who would know what to do in this situation. It's no use. I'm just a kid and the hat isn't even really a hat any more, more a tangle of straw. I think back to the last time I was wearing it, when the boat crashed into us. I had Mum's sunglasses on then too, but who knows where they are.

That's what made me realise. I was wearing Mum's hat and sunglasses. I'm nearly as tall as she is. For all the people on the other boat knew, *I* could have been Mum.

Things are slowly starting to fall into place in my head. My fingers are tingling with panic.

They weren't trying to kill me, they were trying to kill Mum.

Which means that she's still in danger.

A knot is growing in the pit of my stomach. I have to find a way off this island. Not just

for me any more, but for Mum, Dad and Olly.
I can't let anything hurt them.

Afternoon

Something terrible has happened. Even worse
than the fire being put out.

As I made my way back into the jungle, I
heard a shriek and a thud. I knew instantly that
it was Goldie. A sudden dreadful heaviness
filled my heart.

'Goldie!' I screamed. I rushed through the
trees, parting the branches, leaping over the
ground, sweat running down my face with
the last bits of rain. 'Where are you?' There was
silence apart from my breaths, loud and
rasping.

I stared up into our tree, into the branches.
She wasn't there.

Then I heard a whimper and looked down. A

small bundle of fur lay on the ground, covered in mud and twigs. Goldie. I knelt next to her. She opened her eyes and climbed on to my lap. She kept her right long arm tucked in to her body, not moving it. She must have hurt it.

'It's OK,' I said softly. 'You're going to be just fine.' She seemed soothed by my voice and I gently hugged her to my chest.

I glanced up. She must have slipped on one of the wet branches and fallen out of the tree. She was just a baby, still learning. She'd probably never lived in this kind of forest before. There weren't any other gibbons around to teach her what to do. There were some monkeys, some macaques. I could tell they were monkeys because they had tails. But no gibbons. I had to get her help.

I knew that Goldie longed to be in the trees, that she feels safest there. So I climbed as high as I could and held her in my arms, rocking back and forth and cradling her. 'You have to be OK,' I said to her.

We were connected. We needed each other.

Two-ish hours later

After the rain stopped completely, I cried for a long time. Things have really fallen apart today.

Goldie is hurt.

Someone is trying to kill Mum.

All my hard work – my help signs, my fire signal – have been washed away in the storm.

If it wasn't for Goldie needing my help then I think I would have given up. But I couldn't let her down. She was sleeping in my arms; she trusted me.

I wiped away my tears and thought about what she would need when she woke up. Food. And water.

I placed her carefully in a safe nook in the

tree, then climbed down and retrieved one of the clam shells that had collected water during the storm. I left it at the base of the tree.

Now I'm going to head out into the jungle, looking for any fruit that has been knocked off the trees by the storm. This is the only thing I can think to do that might help her.

Thirty-ish minutes later

I've seen something. Something that could change everything. I had almost made it to Lizard Beach before I spotted Goldie's favourite almond fruit, high up in the canopy above me. I scrambled up a fallen tree trunk to get to them. As I did, I gazed through the trees across the sea to the North Island and I noticed something I hadn't seen before. Butterflies filled my stomach. In the distance, two pointy stone towers poked up above the trees. There's a building on North Island. And a building means people.

I'm trying to not get my hopes up.

There's still the small problem of crossing the jellyfish-infested waters.

There's the chance we get there and it turns out to be an abandoned building.

But if I can find a way to get us there, we might be saved . . .

Full-moon, evening

I've decided to build a raft; it's the only way I can get us across the sea to the North Island. While I was close to Lizard Beach, I gathered everything I might need. The storm had washed all sorts up along the sand: rope, string, and hundreds of plastic bottles. The rope and string I'd need to hold the raft together, and the bottles would help it float. I didn't need it to stay together for long, just long enough to make it across the jellyfish waters.

After a while I found fishing net, fallen bamboo and driftwood. I'd use that for the main body of the raft, for Goldie and me to sit on. I collected about fifty plastic bottles and trapped them in a fishing net, ready to attach them to the bottom of the raft.

I worked as quickly as I could, as daylight was disappearing.

A few minutes later, I gazed back into the jungle. It already looked too dark to see my way through, and I decided it was time to leave. After making sure all my supplies wouldn't blow away or get swept away by the tide if another storm raged through, I raced back through the jungle, ignoring every creak of wood, animal growl, and crunch of leaves that I passed.

As I got closer, I felt the familiar feeling of

being watched and glanced up to see Goldie limping along a branch, still clutching her arm close to her. I raced up to her.

'You're awake,' I said to her.

She jumped into my arms and hugged me tightly and I clasped her close to me. She chattered away, as if telling me all about her fall. My body filled with relief that she seemed to be all right. Soon we'd be rescued together. Everything was finally working out.

'Wait till you see what we're doing,' I said, handing her one of the almond-like fruits. 'We're going on an adventure together.'

She looked up at me with her big brown eyes and I smiled at her. Out of the jungle, on the beach, it was still light enough to see. I wanted to check if anything else had washed up on this side that we might need.

I placed Goldie on a branch but she climbed straight back on to my arm.

'You can come with me,' I said and she sat down on my shoulder, her legs dangling down my back.

There were many of the same things washed up on this beach, bits of plastic and big splinters of wood. I saw something white floating at the water's edge and I moved closer and bent down to have a look. It was a piece of broken deck chair, I think. Nothing useful. As soon as I got close to the water, Goldie wriggled and screeched, wanting to get away. I tried to hold her gently, to stop her from leaping into the water or hurting herself, but it was no good. I quickly backed away out of the waves and let her go and she limped back to the trees.

I sighed and watched her go. I had a new problem to think about.

How was I going to get Goldie on the raft?

It reminded me of when Olly was two and he'd go full dead weight if he didn't want to get in his car seat. There was nothing Mum could do but wait for him to be ready. I needed to do that with Goldie.

The problem was, I didn't know if she'd ever be ready to get on the raft. I knew why she was scared of water. I understood more than anyone. She peeked out of the branches and looked down at me.

'I get it,' I said to her. 'I know that you're scared. I'm scared too.'

She seemed to be listening, to be understanding, but she didn't come down. There's not much light left now. Tomorrow we'll need to trek through the jungle first thing, I'll build the raft on the beach, and then I'll find some way of getting Goldie to come on to it with me.

Maybe by this time tomorrow we'll have found help on the other island, and everything will OK.

DAY 9

To do today:

1. Build the raft and persuade Goldie to get on it
2. Get rescued!

Mid-morning

We're on Lizard Beach. I've made the raft. It's down by the water's edge. I've tested it on the sand and it holds my weight. All that's left is to get on it. I don't even need to worry about how to get Goldie on to the raft any more, she's too weak to protest.

When Goldie woke up at dawn today, she didn't sing. That's when I knew that something was really wrong. Her fur seemed dull and damp. I couldn't lose her. I cried, my tears wetting her soft fur.

It took me hours to build the raft. I wish that I'd made it sooner. I should have tried to make it to the other island earlier – before things got so bad.

The raft looks solid enough. I hope it will work. It's basically three logs tied together in a triangle with hundreds of plastic bottles underneath and bamboo and fishing net in the middle. I'm planning to use the piece of driftwood that looks like a bone as an oar.

I've put everything I want to bring with us in the washed-up bag I found.

I packed:

- The tin can
- Bottles of rain water
- My flip flop

- My T-shirt hat
- Rope
- My clam-knife
- My notebook, jammed inside a big plastic bottle to keep it dry
- The glasses
- The pens

Now I'm ready. I've been delaying actually getting on to the raft because I'm scared. I'm scared that it won't float, or that it'll fall apart halfway across and the jellyfish will sting me. But I can't delay any more. I *have* to try. Not just for me. For Goldie.

Afternoon, the North Island

Well, we made it. Barely.

Before leaving, I slipped my arms through the bright orange life jacket and fastened it around my waist, grateful to have it with me. I assembled a sling out of the T-shirt that I'd been using as a hat, and slid Goldie inside it, hoping that she wouldn't be too scared at travelling on the raft if she couldn't see it. She curled up and nuzzled into my chest. I took a deep breath and climbed on to the raft. It bobbed in the water. Goldie stirred but I stroked her and she calmed again. The water was clear and still. I'd be able to keep an eye out for Belladonna the jellyfish.

As we left, tears dripped down my face. Fear pumped around my body. At the same time, I was excited to be on the move, and filled with new energy. A new sense of purpose.

We drifted further out into the water, and I tried to navigate towards the other island, but the waves were taking me where they wanted, pulling me back and forth in the current. My oar didn't do anything. I was getting swept towards the open ocean – a tiny dot, moving under the windswept clouds. Maybe we'd be swept across the world on the currents. Was that even possible?

My knots and ropes were already coming undone. One of the plastic bottles had broken free and bobbed away into the ocean. I plunged my hands into the water and tried to tighten the ropes, calculating how many more bottles I could lose before the raft sank. It wasn't many. Shapes and shadows twisted in the deep water below me.

I couldn't let us be taken out to sea. There was only one thing for it. I placed Goldie carefully in the centre of the raft, still wrapped up, and slid into the water behind her. I held the back log and kicked, propelling the raft forward and hoping we'd passed the jellyfish area.

I was about halfway between the islands when I spotted a fin sticking out of the water. My pulse raced. I tried to steer away by kicking harder but it weaved closer to me, a dark grey dorsal fin.

A shark.

I told myself that it wouldn't hurt me. That it was just swimming in the ocean, its home. But I didn't believe my own words. Then I felt something brush my feet and shrieked. I decided I'd rather be swept out to sea than be a shark's dinner. I heaved myself fully on to the raft, trying to not make sudden jerky movements, keeping one eye on the shark at the same time.

The shark fin circled, then disappeared and I breathed a sigh of relief. After everything that I'd been through, being eaten by a shark couldn't be my ending.

The wind picked up again and the current tugged my little raft. All I could do was hold on and hope that it took us in the right direction. My island was getting smaller and smaller. It was too late to turn back. I could only keep going forward. I tried paddling with my oar again, and, somehow, this time, it felt like I was moving in the right direction. Maybe now that I was closer to the other island, the currents were helping me. I paddled harder and harder, putting all my strength into it.

Finally, after ages, my arms burning and hands sore, I looked down and saw the ocean floor. With a yelp of joy, I jumped off the raft and pushed us the rest of the way to the island. The first thing I did after arriving was to pull the raft up on to the beach and just lie starfished on the sand for a while, recovering. I'd made it. My feet were cut and bleeding from scrambling over the seabed and my arms ached, but I was alive.

Goldie peeked out of my T-shirt and I offered her some water poured from one of the bottles into the palm of my hand. She squeaked at me and I felt my breathing relax. Goldie had perked up. She cupped the water in to her mouth with her left hand, carefully keeping her right arm close to her, then climbed on to my head, standing on the back of my neck.

'Let's see if we can find you some food,' I said. But I sat still for a few minutes more. My legs felt like jelly. Goldie however seemed to be feeling a bit better after the water and crawled down on to my lap and blinked, looking around us at our new surroundings, so eventually I got up too, and took stock of this new island.

I noticed that there was less rubbish washed up on this beach. If we didn't find help, it would be hard to survive here. I glanced down at my own bony body. It was almost unrecognisable. I clutched my bag of items from the South Island close to my chest.

We had to find help here. There was no other option.

I can tell it's going to get dark soon though,

so getting rescued will have to wait until tomorrow. I won't be able to find the building without daylight. I'll have to explore the beach and the treeline for a good sleeping tree.

Evening

I've found a good tree to spend the night in later, one with low thick branches. I was scared to go too high up, scared that I would slip or that Goldie would fall out again. It's still been too cloudy to start a fire but I've put the water bottles out in case it rains.

I want my familiar tree on the other island. Really, I don't want to be in a tree at all.

Still, I need to do what is best for Goldie. And at least we're one step closer to getting rescued.

Night

I don't feel tired tonight, even with the sun setting in a big orange ball on the horizon, sending bright pinks and reds streaking across the sky. The storm clouds have finally lifted. It's nice to be able to see the sunset over the horizon from this North Island; on my island I only really saw the sunrise. This beach faces west and my beach faced east. My stomach is growling and I realise that with all the focus on the crossing and finding a safe place to sleep, I haven't checked for food on this island yet. I think I see some fruit in some of the trees below.

Hold on, I'm going to leave Goldie for a few seconds to investigate.

A few minutes later

This island has banana plants on it! Can you believe it? They're the tiniest and greenest bananas I've ever seen but I couldn't be happier. I had to use my clam-knife to chop them down. They taste kind of bland and starchy but at least this means no more boiled snails for me! They've cheered Goldie up too. She's sitting next to me in this tree munching on one.

There's another thing. I could tell some bananas had been picked off the trees before I got there. It might be monkeys . . . or is this another sign that there really are people here? I'm scared to get my hopes up, but between the building I spotted and the missing bananas, I think there's a chance.

I'm staring up at the stars now, writing by moonlight. The clouds have cleared and

somehow the stars seem extra bright and twinkly after the storm.

DAY 10

To do today:

   1. Find the towers!

Dawn

This morning, even though Goldie was still limping and only using one arm, she stood on her branch and opened her mouth to greet the day. Goldie's song went on for ages, longer than usual. I wondered if it was because we were in a new place. My mouth was so dry that I could hardly join in. But I'm grateful that she's feeling well enough to sing.

Morning

I've been exploring the island all morning searching for the building I saw. So far there's no sign of it. Could I have imagined it? Like a mirage?

I carried Goldie most of the time as she's still not walking normally but I didn't chatter to her like I usually do. I was too focused on looking for signs of human life. To the right of where we landed mangroves grew in swampy waters. I was scared of what might be in them. What if there were crocodiles here?

I turned and walked the length of the beach in the other direction. There were paths in the sand leading from the beach into the jungle. I wasn't sure if they'd been made by people or large animals, but it definitely felt like *something* had been here before.

I followed one of the paths through the

jungle with Goldie hanging on to my back until I came to another beach. It was tiny but the most beautiful beach I'd ever seen, with perfect tiny shells dotting the warm golden sand. From the direction of the sun, I could tell it faced east. Which meant the beach we'd landed on faced west. I've nicknamed them Sunrise and Sunset Beach.

A few minutes later, I think

I'm not sure how long I've been lying in the sand. I'm sitting up now, waiting for the dizziness to subside. I can remember everything that led up to me opening my eyes up from the ground . . .

Even though the beach was beautiful, there was still no sign of human life. And the building seemed to have vanished. I was getting worried that it was a mistake coming to this island and I was feeling panicky about Goldie still being injured.

Then I saw a path in the distance, wide and well-trodden, with vines and bushes pushed out of the way. An actual dirt trail through the jungle.

So I started to run.

And that's how I ended up fainting on the beach.

I woke with a racing heart, staring straight up at the clouds and the piercing sun. Goldie was sitting on my chest, picking things from my hair. She squeaked as I groaned and moved. It was a lucky thing that I'd fainted there and not as I was climbing a tree or clambering over the rocks. That was my lesson learnt.

My head has stopped spinning. It's time for attempt number two at following the trail. We're about to find the building, I know it, I just have to go slowly even though I'm desperate to race there. Days of barely any food are catching up to me. I need to listen to my body. Otherwise I'll be no help to me or Goldie. She's run ahead, under the cover of the trees.

A minute ago I even thought I heard voices in the distance. But I can't tell if they're really there or just in my head.

late afternoon

I can't believe what has just happened.

As I stood up, I realised I really could hear voices. Before I had a chance to shout, I spotted movement in the jungle. Two people wearing caps and long shorts, striding along the well-trodden path towards us. Goldie had been exploring, walking around on the ground on two legs, still unable to swing through the trees and I watched as they stopped and noticed her.

My heart leapt. We were saved!

But I was wrong.

It all happened so quickly. Before I had a chance to shout that I was there I saw one of the people lift up a cage with bananas inside. I watched Goldie use her good arm to do a big swing towards them and then one of the men grabbed her.

Her body writhed and wriggled, trying to escape, trying to get back to me. She squeaked and shrieked. Through the trees I could see the people holding Goldie tightly and stuffing her inside the cage.

Shock turned to anger and I raced towards them. As I reached the trees though, I felt arms close around my body from behind. I opened my mouth to scream but a hand clamped over my face, pushing my scream back in. The person's body wrapped around me and we thudded to the ground.

A voice whispered in my ear. 'Don't make a

sound. If they find us they'll kill us.'

I recognised the voice. A girl's voice.

'Vanna?' I asked, my voice muffled through her hand.

She let go and I rolled over. It *was* Vanna. She raised a finger to her lips, keeping her other hand on my mouth.

The people turned and marched back down the path.

'Don't go after them,' she said. 'They'll hurt you. They'll kill you. They're the men who tried to kill us. OK?'

I nodded, but I wasn't going to stand there doing nothing while poor injured Goldie was taken away. I stood up, looking for Goldie through the trees. She was in the cage, being carried in the opposite direction. I took a step after her but Vanna grabbed my hand and held me back.

'What are you doing?' she hissed.

'I have to get her back,' I replied.

'You can't,' said Vanna. 'It's too dangerous.'

I watched the men disappear into the jungle, realising she was right. If I tried to grab the cage now they'd probably catch me too. I needed a plan. I looked at Vanna properly for the first time. Her face was scratched and her clothes ripped, but it was definitely Vanna. The same Vanna I'd called for every day, the same Vanna I'd thought was lost – or worse. Questions raced through my mind. Had she been here the whole time? What had she been doing? Did she know who the men were? I needed to hear her story. I had to find out what was going on. The more information I had, the more likely it was that I could rescue Goldie.

'Tell me everything,' I said.

'I will,' she said. 'But it's not safe here. Follow me.'

She crept through the jungle back towards

the Sunset Beach, sticking to the shadows. It took ages and I followed behind, feeling completely disorientated. Finally, she stopped at a wooden tent structure covered in palm fronds.

'Have you been here the whole time?' I asked sharply, eyeing up the camp. She must have built it herself. It was way better than my treehouse.

Vanna nodded. 'Were you on the other island?' she asked.

'Yeah,' I said. 'I built a raft to come over.'

'I had a feeling you were there and I wanted to cross to find you, but there were box jellyfish in the water. They're deadly. I couldn't risk it.' Vanna's eyes widened as she talked about the jellyfish.

I shivered. I *knew* that Belladonna the jellyfish was dangerous. It's a good thing I didn't know *how* dangerous or I probably wouldn't have made the crossing. Maybe that would have been a good thing though. At least I'd still have Goldie.

'Who are those people?' I said. 'And why were they waiting with a cage to trap Goldie? How did they know we were here?'

I wasn't sure I trusted Vanna yet, and, after days of not knowing anything and trying to piece the puzzle together I was determined to learn everything as quickly as possible so I could go rescue Goldie.

'They must have heard the gibbon howling this morning,' said Vanna. 'Same as me. I knew they'd try and find you. It's taken me all day to track you down though.' Vanna perched on a log seat and put her head in her hands. She looked like she was feeling dizzy.

'I have water,' I said, offering my bottle.

We sat down side by side on a log bench she'd built. She took the bottle and sipped and then, slowly, finally, she told me her story.

'I guess the first thing to know is that the men who tried to kill us are smugglers. They own this island. This is where they bring gibbons and other animals they've captured before they're smuggled over the ocean.'

'So Bora was right about it all?' I asked.

Vanna nodded.

'But . . . why did you have a gibbon on your boat?' I asked. I didn't want to believe that Vanna was working with the smugglers, but what other explanation was there?

She took a deep breath in before speaking again. 'I never meant to get caught up in all of this, you know,' she said. 'It just happened. About six months ago, I was getting Bora's boat ready when a woman approached me and asked if I could transport her pet. She said that it was a secret. She offered me money. Lots of money.'

I scoffed but continued listening.

'I thought it would be a cat or a dog or something! But it was a baby gibbon in a cage. I'd already spent some of the money.' Vanna stuttered. 'I-I didn't know what to do so . . . I just did what they told me. I brought the gibbon to their headquarters on this island.'

I felt a sudden rush of emotions. Anger that Vanna had been helping to smuggle gibbons for so long. Confusion that she was helping me now. And worry about what was going to happen to Goldie now that I knew she'd been captured by smugglers.

'So why are you hiding from them?' I asked suspiciously.

'Because I don't want to be helping them! Once I took the first gibbon, they told me there would be more. They wouldn't let me get out of it,' Vanna continued. 'They said that if I told anyone or ever stopped doing it, they'd harm uncle Bora and my family but looking back, I should have done more . . . found a way to get help or stop them somehow.'

I felt myself soften slightly.

'That's awful. I'm sorry.'

'*I'm* sorry. I'm so sorry for everything,' said Vanna. 'But if we can get off this island and find your mum, I have evidence that she can use to expose the smugglers. I want them to be stopped. Do you . . . do you think we could work together?'

I thought for a long time. I didn't like what Vanna had done but I wondered if I would have done anything differently if I was in her shoes. And it seemed like she really was genuinely sorry and did want to do the right thing now.

'OK,' I said finally, and I held out my hand. She shook it with both of hers and then we hugged. 'But we're not leaving without Goldie,' I said. 'That gibbon was my friend the whole time I was on the other island. I wouldn't be alive without her. I can't leave her behind.'

So we're going to get Goldie back together. I'm organising my bag before we leave. The clam-knife is awkward to walk with so I'm leaving it behind with the tin can but I'm bringing everything else. And I'm wearing the life jacket, in case I need it. You never know.

Night

Our rescue mission is going well so far. We've made it across the whole island and are close to where Goldie is being held captive.

It was another tough journey. The smuggling headquarters are on the very north of the island. To get here we had to walk through the forest and then along the beach back to the well-trodden path and *then* climb over rocks. The journey gave me a chance to get to know Vanna a bit better though and to understand more about how we've ended up here.

'I can't believe that you were here the whole time I was on that island,' I said to Vanna, as we walked through the forest. 'Didn't you hear me shouting?'

She shook her head. 'I wish I had.'

'Why do the smugglers bring the gibbons here?' I asked.

'No one comes here. So they can hide the gibbons in the headquarters while they're waiting for them to be taken away by boat to other countries and smuggled across borders. Or worse,' she said under her breath.

My skin crawled at the evilness of it all.

'This northern island is big,' said Vanna. 'I'm warning you. It's going to take us a while to get there.'

'We won't stop. We won't stop walking until we find them, OK?' I said. 'Until we reach the headquarters.'

She gave me a firm nod.

We battled our way through a wall of dense undergrowth. To me, everything looked the same. I could hardly see up to the sky so didn't even have the sun to guide me. We could have just been going round and round in circles for all I knew.

Vanna seemed to know where we were going though, and we eventually made it to the beach. From the edge of the jungle, she peered out at the open ocean, searching for smuggler boats. Once she was satisfied no one would see us, she gestured at me to follow her, but she said we'd have to keep close to the treeline and the shadows. I could tell Vanna was nervous.

We reached the well-trodden path and I raced towards it, but Vanna shook her head.

'It's too dangerous to go along that path,' she whispered. 'The smugglers sometimes hunt at night there.'

'What do they hunt?' I asked.

'Frogs,' she said and then pointed to the north of the beach. 'The next beach is beyond those boulders. We'll have to climb over them during low tide. We have to time it just right.'

Vanna pulled some fallen palm fronds from the jungle floor and dragged them on to the thin sliver of beach. 'Here,' she said, gesturing at me to sit down. 'It will be a while before the tide goes out.'

We sat down next to each other and listened to the roar of the waves.

Something moved beneath my feet. It was bigger than a crab. I jumped up and darted out of the way then bent over to look. It was hard to see in the dark and I was grateful for the clear sky and the big moon.

'Are these . . . ?' I asked.

'Turtle hatchlings!' said Vanna.

I watched as the tiny turtles scuttled as fast

as they could over the sand and into the sea. A bird flew above them, poised and ready to snatch. I flapped my arms and shooed it away. I watched as another turtle got stuck trying to climb over a log and fell on to its back. It struggled until it was the right way up again, and then raced into the waves. I wanted to make a path for the sea turtles to go straight into the sea without any obstacles but Vanna dragged me back into the shelter of the jungle.

'Look, you can see them ride the waves for a second before they disappear,' said Vanna, pointing.

'Good luck, little turtles,' I said.

'Did you know that they'll return here to nest in a few years when they're ready to have eggs?' asked Vanna.

I shook my head. 'How do they find their way home?'

'I don't know. Uncle Bora says that they can

smell the beach, the island.' She took a deep breath in.

I sniffed but could only smell and taste the salty air. 'I didn't know it had a smell.'

'Everything has a smell,' said Vanna. 'But I read that they also have a kind of internal magnetic compass.'

I glanced at the tide, anxious to keep going. It was still too high.

'You know coral sings so that the fish can find it. Maybe the beach sings to the turtles,' said Vanna.

I smiled at her. 'I like that idea.'

'I always slow my boat down when I'm close to the coast. I don't know if it makes a difference but what if the boat noise interferes with something, you know?'

Vanna seemed to care so deeply about some animals – yet she had been involved with the smugglers. I wondered what would have happened if I'd never made it to this island. Would she have tried to take down the smugglers herself?

'What was your plan before I got here?' I asked.

'I was still figuring that out.' She peered out at the waves and then stood up. 'Come, we can cross now. The tide's out.'

I stared at the rocks we needed to cross, illuminated by moonlight. Even with the low tide, the rocks weren't fully out of the water. There were three big boulders the same height and a giant one, much taller. When a wave came in, the sea smashed against the boulders, swirling and whirling and completely submerging the smaller three.

Vanna waited for a wave to recede and then maneuvered across the rocks on all fours before climbing up on to the giant boulder, safe from the next surge of water. I put my foot on the first rock to follow her. It was wet and slippery. There was no way I could go as quickly as Vanna had. I knelt, gripped on to the edge of the rocks and shimmied along. There was only a few seconds before the next wave would crash into me. I found a hold in the giant boulder to pull myself up – but I didn't do it in time. The wave knocked my feet out from under me and I slipped against the rock with a thud. Salty water engulfed me. The lifejacket stopped my body from slamming into the rocks below.

'Lark!' Vanna called.

She jumped down and grabbed my hand, yanking me out from the water. The waves swirled around us.

'Quickly,' she said and she gave me a foot up so I could climb on to the higher rock before scrabbling up herself. I lay on my back on the boulder, gasping for breath. Just when I thought I'd got the better of the island, something like that happened.

We lay next to each other. 'Are you OK?' I asked.

'I think so,' she said and checked her body for cuts. 'How about you?'

'I'm OK,' I said shakily. I turned to face her. 'Thanks for helping me. We've got to find the gibbons and get off this island before anything else happens.'

She nodded, but looked worried. 'What are you going to do once we're at their headquarters?' Vanna asked.

'I don't know,' I replied, watching the sky and the trees blow in the wind above me. A seabird floated on the upwind. 'Take Goldie and run, I guess. I figured I'd think of something when we got there.'

Vanna rubbed her hands against her face. 'These are dangerous people, Lark, remember?' she said. 'They tried to kill us. We need a plan.

You can't just run in!'

'I'm not stupid,' I said. 'I won't get us caught. Not when Goldie's life is at risk.' The thought of seeing the smugglers filled me with fear, but I was also angry, angrier than I'd ever felt before. The smugglers had come after Mum and now Goldie.

'You know I don't think they were trying to kill *me*. They thought I was my mum because I was wearing her hat,' I said, suddenly realising that Vanna wouldn't know that. 'They weren't trying to kill me on the boat, they were trying to kill my mum.'

Vanna froze and nodded slowly, making sense of it all. 'They'd still try to hurt you now though.' She spoke with a warning tone. 'You've seen too much.'

'I know,' I said. 'I'll be careful.'

'We're almost there,' said Vanna. 'Should we keep going?'

I nodded but didn't move. 'I need a second,' I said.

We'd been moving all night long and the first hints of morning birdsong sounded through the darkness.

'How did they know so much about Mum?' I asked. The one question that I couldn't get out of my mind. 'Were you involved in them trying to kill her?'

'Of course not!' she said, sounding offended. 'I never thought they'd do something like that. My job was to deliver gibbons to the island and the mainland. Then they started asking questions about the woman coming to see Uncle Bora – your mum. I did tell them he was meeting your mum that afternoon and the next morning.' She stuttered. 'I thought the fact someone was investigating the disappearing gibbons might scare them into stopping . . .'

Disbelief flashed through me, red hot and

rising. 'They knew who she was and where she would be, thanks to you.' I stood up shakily. 'You were going to get my mum killed.'

Vanna looked away and swallowed. 'I didn't think they were going to . . . going to hurt her. I didn't realise how dangerous they were. I'm so sorry.'

I was crying now. 'I need to find Goldie and then get off this island!' I said. I wiped my eyes and climbed down from the boulder on to the beach. Vanna followed me and we continued onwards. I strode ahead, kicking at the stones beneath my feet. This thin part of the beach was covered in pebbles. I must have been going the right way because it was ages before Vanna stopped me, where the beach ended and the only place to continue was through the jungle.

'Lark,' she said. 'Lark!' She caught up to me. 'Hey, we haven't eaten in hours. Have a banana.'

I took it reluctantly and peeled it. Some of

my anger drained away with each bite.

'Let me make it right,' said Vanna. 'I'm so sorry this happened. I keep going over everything in my head and wishing I'd done things differently.'

'Me too,' I said. I realised there was no point being angry right now. What good would it do? If there's anything I've learnt on this island it's that anger at a situation doesn't do anything – not on its own. You have to be willing to act, to make things better. I took a sip of water.

'I see you, anger,' I murmured to myself. 'But now's not a good time.' I took a deep breath and felt the rage and stiffness in my body subside. I needed to focus on action, on getting Goldie back and then getting off this island so that I could warn Mum, Dad and Olly.

I smiled at Vanna and noticed silent tears dripping down her cheeks.

'It's not your fault, Vanna,' I said, seeing

how much she was blaming herself for all of this. 'It's them. *They* tried to kill us. And you're just a kid who they roped into this. It's not your fault,' I said again.

Vanna sniffed loudly and wiped her nose. I threw my arms around her and gave her a hug. After a while I let go and she smiled at me.

'Should we keep going?' I asked.

She nodded. 'We'll need to wait until it gets fully light before we go into the jungle though. Otherwise we'll have no chance of seeing where we're going.'

That's where we are now. At the edge of the jungle, waiting for sunrise. I'm curled up on the sand, watching the sky. It's strange to not have Goldie with me. I never thought I'd miss sleeping in a tree.

Vanna's next to me though, and, together, we're watching the last of the stars disappear, the sky preparing for a new day.

DAY 11

To do today:

1. Rescue Goldie

Dawn

We had just re-entered the jungle when we heard a ship horn, low and loud. We glanced at each other, mouths open in disbelief, and then we were both racing through the trees back to the beach. There, out across the waves, silhouetted by the rising sun, was a big boat.

'Is that the smugglers?' I asked.

Vanna shook her head. 'No, they never use boats that big. That's some kind of passenger ferry, I think. I wonder what it's doing out here.'

Our rescue.

Our way off the island.

We threw our hands into the air and waved. I slid the glasses out of my pocket and knelt in the sand and tried to start a fire so that they would see the smoke but the sun wasn't high enough in the sky.

'They're not going to see us!' I shouted desperately.

'We can swim out to it,' said Vanna. 'Or use your raft?'

'It's way back on the other beach. Besides, it's falling apart,' I said. Then another thought entered my mind. I couldn't leave now. There was no way I could abandon Goldie here, in that cage. I could still see her scared eyes peeking out between the bars, searching for me.

I knew it in my heart that Goldie was close. I heard it on the whisper of the wind that I had to rescue her.

'I can't leave,' I said.

Vanna looked confused.

'Mum always said that one day I'd find something important that I really care about and understand why her work matters so much.' I stood tall and looked Vanna in the eyes, more confident than I've ever felt in my life. 'Well, I've found it. It's Goldie. You go,' I said to Vanna. 'Take my notebook and swim out to them. Tell them everything. I'll find Goldie.'

Vanna hesitated for a second, clearly unsure what to do.

'It's OK,' I reassured her. 'My notebook explains everything that happened to me. Give it to the rescuers so they know to come back and get help for me and Goldie. Keep it in the plastic bag and maybe put it in a plastic bottle too, to be extra safe.'

She nodded slowly. 'I'll draw you a map to the headquarters quickly,' she said. 'They look like temple ruins. You'd never guess anyone was living there.' This must have been the building I'd spotted from the other island.

I nodded my thanks and she quickly scribbled a map in the notebook. I ripped the page out along with a few others and stuffed them in my pocket.

I slipped off the lifejacket and handed it to Vanna. 'You'll need this,' I said and helped her thread her arms through.

The ship blew its horn again.

'Go!' I said, pressing the notebook into her palm. 'While you still have time.'

She squeezed my hands and smiled at me and then turned and ran back to the water and dived in.

Afternoon

I only have four pieces of paper left from the pages I ripped out of the notebook. And there's a lot that happened since Vanna left, so I'm going to write very small. I tried to write earlier but I couldn't stop crying and the tears made the paper soggy so I had to stop. Now I'm not crying. Or at least I'm not letting the tears drip on to the paper.

After Vanna jumped into the water, I wanted to stay and make sure she made it to the boat safely, but I knew I couldn't waste any time. The smugglers could have been planning to take Goldie from the island at any moment. So instead I turned back to the jungle and followed Vanna's map.

I made it to the temple pretty quickly, though the landscape by the headquarters was different, swampier than other places on the island, with thick, nearly impenetrable jungle. I got as close as I could while still staying hidden in the foliage, and then laid down on my stomach and watched through parted ferns. Ants crawled over my legs and I had to stop myself from shrieking at the creepy-crawly feeling.

In front of me was a crumbling ancient temple that had been taken over by trees. One tree was growing directly over the entrance, its roots coming down on either side of the door, making an archway. Columns wrapped with vines stood at the front. Carvings were barely visible in the walls underneath. The rock was the same colour as the dusty earth around it.

On top of the temple stood four pointed stone towers, one in each corner, with carvings of faces on them. The tower furthest away had fallen on to its side and another was leaning as much as the Leaning Tower of Pisa. Then there were the trees. Huge roots, three times as thick as me, grew into the roof and down the side of the temple. It was as if the temple was being swallowed by the jungle.

As I was wondering if I could risk getting any closer, I heard footsteps thundering along the path. I ducked even lower but kept watching. Two men were walking along the path to the entrance of the temple. I only saw them from a distance but I recognised them instantly with their caps and long shorts. They were the men from the boat, the ones who had crashed into us – and the same ones who had taken Goldie. They disappeared inside.

I decided I couldn't risk getting closer so instead I did what Goldie would do: I climbed a tree to get a better look. I perched on a branch, overlooking the roof of the crumbling temple. Only one half had a roof any more – that must be where the gibbons were being kept. It was covered in green moss.

I could see the men walking through a courtyard. One had a long-sleeved T-shirt the exact deep red colour of the centipede with red legs from the jungle. I named him Centipede at first, but then I thought it was unfair to centipedes to name a smuggler after them, so I decided to call him Crawler. The other one had a green camouflage T-shirt which reminded me of the trees. I glanced down at my scratched arms and legs and decided on Scratcher. They went down a long open corridor, then they reached a doorway, switched on a noisy generator and turned right out of sight into the temple.

The ruins made me think of Olly's wooden blocks, with all the stones piled up on top of each other. Some looked like they were balancing precariously, only held in place by the vines and tree roots.

With the men disappeared inside the covered

part of the building, I thought it was safe to go a bit nearer, so I climbed down and inched closer until I was sitting on top of the outer wall. Even the intact part of the roof looked delicate, so I carefully crouched on my hands and knees to peek down through the cracks.

I was looking into what seemed like a living area. The men were in there, bent over a camping stove. One held a pot in his hand. I saw two camping beds and chairs and a little kitchen area with clay mugs and stainless-steel pots, pans and plates.

There was also a big container of water. Litres and litres of it. Clean, fresh water. The kind I hadn't had in days. It made me a million times thirstier but I told myself not to get distracted. I couldn't see any sign of Goldie and the gibbons. They must be in a different room. I wasn't exactly sure what my rescue plan would be, but I figured the first step was to find where Goldie was being kept.

I edged along the corner of the roof, watching the men eat and chat below me. My heart thumped loudly. It was dark in there but they had lights from the generator. At least the thrum of the generator would cover the sound of my movement. The air was filled with the smell of a camping gas stove and the sizzle of cooking fish.

I stood and balanced on the edge of the roof. I continued walking until I was overlooking the next room over. Through the cracks in the roof flashed the metal of a cage.

My stomach turned. That's where Goldie had to be. I wanted to whistle, to let her know that I was going to rescue her. But I couldn't risk the men hearing.

I looked around, trying to work out how to get there from the ground.

The entrance to the covered part of the

building was from the open courtyard I'd seen the men walking through. A long hallway seemed to lead from there to the other rooms of the temple.

I'd have to get into the courtyard, enter the hallway and then go left. That would be the most direct way. But that would mean I'd have to walk past the doorway of the room the men were in.

I tip-toed back along the roof towards the first room, wanting to check whether the men might have left, but as I approached, I stepped too near to a crumbing hole, and a stone fell and clattered noisily down the inside of the temple. I froze. The men's voices stopped. I heard movement.

I shimmied backwards, trying to be as silent as possible. I peered through a gap in the stones to see what the men were doing and shrieked as Crawler's two eyes stared back at me. He shouted something I didn't understand.

I ran, jumping across the roof until I was at the edge of the building, then I leapt into one of the trees, hiding in the foliage.

I peeked through the leaves, my heart pounding as the men came running out of the temple and fanned out into the surrounding jungle to look for me.

I took deep breaths and tried to think of the best thing to do.

They clearly didn't know where I was. Maybe now was my chance to get Goldie, as they were both out of the temple.

I'd have to be quick.

I felt like I was playing a game of 40–40 except the guards were the smugglers and the home base was the gibbon. (Plus the smugglers were probably trying to kill me. But I tried not to think about that part.) I needed to get Goldie and escape with her. I didn't have a plan beyond that.

I counted to three, then shimmied down from the tree and sprinted as fast as I could towards the temple entrance, leaping over vines. Loose pebbles dug in to the soles of my feet. I ducked under the low stone entrance.

It was then that I heard a shout and glanced behind me. They'd spotted me. That wasn't part of the plan. I had a decent head start in front of them. I could still make it to Goldie. But would I make it back out? I'd be running straight towards them. The only thing to do was try. I had my bag with me. Maybe I could trap them with the fishing net or something . . .

I ran down the long corridor with the generator in it. Racing to the end, I turned in and then left. I stopped. Passages leading in different directions branched ahead of me. It was dark and felt as if I was in a maze. The temple looked so different down here than from above.

I turned down one of the corridors and ran. Footsteps thudded, but they were still far behind me. I glanced back. The corridor was empty for now. Giant roots snaked along the stones and I had to leap over them.

I turned a corner and realised that it was a dead end.

'No, no, no,' I whispered under my breath. I was trapped.

Touching the cold stone with my fingertips, I desperately looked around. To the side of me, halfway along the corridor, stood a pile of fallen rocks.

The footsteps thudded closer. Crawler and Scratcher were gaining on me.

Then I realised there was a thin shaft of light shining on the top of the pile of rocks. An opening in the roof! I clambered up, knocking over loose stones. Stretching as high as I could, I managed to grip the roof. I heaved myself up, pushing stones out of the way until the hole was big enough and I squeezed out on to the roof.

I had popped out by the fallen tower in the corner of the temple. Stacks of rocks covered the roof. No wonder the roof had caved in one part of the passage.

I peered down. Crawler and Scratcher reached the end of the corridor and pushed against the dead end wall, searching for me. My heart raced. They would soon spot the hole in the roof and realise where I was. They wouldn't make it out of the hole I'd climbed through – not as it was – they were far too big. But they could shift rocks and eventually make it large enough. I had to stop them before they did.

An idea flashed through my mind. I couldn't outrun Crawler and Scratcher, but I could trap them.

I made a split-second plan.

Leaping up, I caught on to an overhanging

branch that was right above the roof line. There was a tower of loose rock in front of me right above the corridor and I wanted to knock it down so that it fell through the hole in the roof and trapped the smugglers underneath in the dead-end part of the passage.

I swung back and forth. When I had enough momentum, I let go and went flying through the air, feet first. My feet bashed in to the pile of rocks, which tumbled over. They hit the roof and crashed through. Success!

But then I lost my balance and began to fall with the rocks, into the passage. I thudded against the cold stone floor. I shielded my head to protect myself from the rocks clattering all around me. A thick dust cloud filled the air and I coughed.

After a few seconds I lifted my head. Behind me, the corridor was now completely blocked. I'd done it! I'd trapped the smugglers. The downside was that I'd blocked the route ahead of me too. I'd have to climb out through the hole in the roof above me, the one I'd made as I fell through.

Except as I reached up to grip the rocks, pain seared up my left wrist and along my arm. I tried again but it hurt so badly I almost passed out. I couldn't climb. I was trapped.

So that's where I am now. Shafts of light shine in from the hole I fell through, but apart from that it's dark, damp and cold. My idea didn't quite go to plan. I'd trapped the smugglers, but I had also trapped myself. I've tried pushing against the fallen stones but they're too heavy to move. I've had another go at climbing back up but my wrist hurts too much. It's not getting better. If anything, it's getting worse. Every now and then I hear more rocks thunder and fall. The tree roots were holding so much of this temple together and it seems like I set off a chain reaction.

I just hope the gibbons are OK.

Evening

I was curled up on the cold floor when I heard a shaky whistle coming from somewhere nearby. I lifted my head.

'Vanna?' I whispered.

'It's me,' she said. Her voice was muffled but close. She was in the temple with me.

'How . . . how are you here?' I asked.

'I got halfway to the boat but then I realised I couldn't leave you here alone,' she said. 'I swam back. I had a feeling something bad might happen.'

'I'm trapped behind the rock and the smugglers are trapped just beyond me,' I said.

'Wait there.' Her voice was closer now. 'I'm coming to you.'

Rocks clattered and echoed.

'It's no good,' said Vanna. 'I can't move the bricks, they're too heavy.'

'There's a hole in the roof,' I said, touching the stones separating Vanna and me. 'Can you reach it?'

'I'll try,' she said.

For ages I heard nothing and then I heard scrambling and climbing above. Vanna's head poked over the roof into the corridor.

'Can you climb out?' she asked.

I showed her my wrist, already swollen and purple.

'I'll come down and you can use my hands as a step. Do you think that will work?'

I nodded and rested my head back against the wall in relief. Vanna jumped down into the corridor.

I put my good arm around her. 'Thank you for coming back.'

Tentatively she put her arms around me in return and for a moment we just stood there, hugging each other. Then Vanna stepped back. 'We should go,' she said. 'Before anything else happens.'

'Wait,' I said. 'I have to check Crawler and Scratcher are alive.'

'Who?' Vanna asked, sounding confused.

'The smugglers,' I explained.

I didn't want to have killed them. I didn't want to hurt *anyone*. I'd only wanted to stop them.

I pulled a small rock from the tower of stones separating us and raised my eye to the opening.

A hand shot through and grabbed on to my bad wrist as I pushed myself away.

'Let me go!' I shouted, pulling – but his grip was too strong.

Vanna prised the stubby fingers off from mine and then we climbed as fast as we could away from them. She helped me up on to the roof. I yelped as I had to use my arm to get over the wall, but I made it.

Vanna scrambled up after me.

'What do we do now?' she asked. 'What about the smugglers?'

'They're still trapped for now,' I replied, glancing down at the rocks below me.

'I don't think we have long until they figure a way out,' said Vanna.

I clasped my hand in Vanna's. 'Let's find Goldie quickly then.'

She squeezed my hand in return and we backtracked to the bit of the roof over the main entrance, then crawled backwards carefully down. I had to climb one-handed. Then we retraced my steps, but more slowly this time, until we found the room I thought had the gibbons in it.

My heart sank when we walked inside. There

was just an empty cage on a table. Vanna pointed to the right. The passageway there sloped downwards, leading deep underground. Silently, we took it. Giant centipedes crawled across the dirt floor.

'I can hardly see,' said Vanna.

At last, we came to a door. I heaved it open, using my good arm. Long shadows stretched across the walls. The room smelled of urine and decay, like a rotting mouse. Inside were eight wire mesh cages, three with gibbons in them. The one at the end had Goldie. I rushed up to her. Her cage was fastened with a clip, which I quickly undid. I opened the cage and took her out.

'Are you OK? It's me, Lark,' I whispered. 'I'm so sorry I left you.'

She clung to my chest, breathing heavily.

I pulled my T-shirt hat from my head and made a sling again for her to sit in so that I could have my hands free. She buried her head inside and whimpered softly.

'It's OK,' I whispered to her and stroked her head. 'I've got you. You're safe now.'

There was a thundering sound above.

'We've got to get out of here,' said Vanna. Her voice quavered. 'I think the temple's collapsing.'

'What about the other two gibbons?' I asked. They both looked a bit bigger than Goldie. I wondered if they were dangerous. I knew from Goldie that gibbons were very strong and if I was them I'd feel pretty frightened by humans at this point.

'Help me push the cages towards the door,' I said, getting an idea and ushering at Vanna to help.

'We haven't got time to carry them outside!' said Vanna, her voice now panicky.

'We won't have to. Just follow my lead. When

I say go, open the cage and then back away behind it, OK?' I said.

She nodded.

'Go!' I shouted and we both opened the cages then flattened ourselves out of the way. The gibbons ran out of the cages on two legs, arms in the air, straight towards the sunlight.

Stones tumbled down around us.

'Quick!' shouted Vanna.

I held Goldie tight to me in the sling and ran, ignoring the stinging pain in my arm and the soles of my feet. Vanna was close behind me.

We made it out, rocks falling around us. The temple was crumbling. I felt a momentary guilt for Crawler and Scratcher, but I knew they wouldn't have cared if it was me. Plus, I couldn't do anything to help them now. The two rescued gibbons darted into the forest and climbed up into the trees, filling the treetops with their howls and songs.

'What now?' I asked.

'The smugglers usually have a boat here,' said Vanna. 'Let's go find it.'

We waded through the mangroves. Snakes swam all around me and I tried not to wonder if they were deadly.

Vanna stopped. 'The boat's not here,' she said. 'Either they left it somewhere else or someone else has it. Which means they might come back. We need to get out of here.'

We turned and quickly headed back towards our Sunset Beach, this time taking the well-trodden path before fighting through the jungle and slumping down on to the sand. My arm still hurt and I was hungry and thirsty, but I smiled at Vanna and she smiled back. We'd made it out of there and I had Goldie, safe and sound – for now, at least.

late evening

We decided we'd be safest back at Vanna's camp, so we spent the rest of the evening travelling there. Now me, Vanna and Goldie are back where we started, at her camp on Sunset Beach on the North Island. Goldie hasn't left my side the whole time.

I wanted to write about everything that had happened as soon as I could.

'Do you have my notebook?' I asked Vanna when we arrived, hot and exhausted. I was running out of space on the pages I'd ripped out.

She shook her head. 'When I decided to swim back to shore, I tied it to the life jacket and a shredded T-shirt I found. I figured that the boat might think it was a person and pick it up.'

Vanna sounded hopeful, but I didn't think that the boat would notice a tiny life jacket in the huge ocean. That's if the bottle and jacket even washed towards them on the waves. So that's it. My notebook is probably lost for ever. At least I have these pages.

'What do we do now?' I asked as I started a fire with the glasses from my bag.

Vanna smiled cheekily. 'Well I don't know about you but I'm starving . . . I stole their food and some of their water when I was looking for you. Let's have a feast.'

We used the tin can to heat up the food over the fire. Fish and rice. I couldn't believe I was going to get to eat something other than fruit. Or snails!

'What's going to be the first thing you eat when you get off the island?' Vanna asked me as the fish cooked.

'Ice cream,' I said. 'And I strangely miss cereal right now.'

Vanna laughed. 'I'm going to have amok,'

she said. 'It's a creamy coconut fish curry. Then I'd have pumpkin custard and banana cake.'

'That sounds good,' I said. 'Although I don't think I'll want to eat coconuts again for a while.'

We laughed together as the food cooked.

So that's what we're doing now, watching the sunset and munching on a real meal! Goldie is sleeping on my chest. She's had all the bananas a baby gibbon could possibly want. This is the last of the notebook pages. We had to use a tiny bit to start the fire. I'm glad I only hurt my left wrist (I've put it in Goldie's sling, which is helping) so that I can still write.

It looks like we'll be on this island tomorrow too but at least we're together now. If we have to keep surviving, I'd rather be a team.

Vanna, Goldie and me.

DAY 12

It was the next morning that we heard a boat engine. At first we hid, thinking that it was the smugglers. But then a siren sounded followed by a loudspeaker shouting our names. I peeked out and saw an official-looking boat – grey with red lines on the side.

'It's the police!' shouted Vanna.

I jumped out of the trees with Goldie holding on to my back and waved my good arm at them. They pulled up to the beach, slowing down and bobbing over the waves. I couldn't believe they were real. Vanna hugged me, tears dripping down her cheeks.

'We're getting rescued!' she said.

I nodded back at her, smiling and shaking my head in disbelief.

We held on to each other and danced in a circle with happiness, the sand soft underneath our toes, as the police officers disembarked.

Goldie climbed on to my front and a butterfly landed on her nose.

The police officers ran towards us through the waves.

Vanna took my hand in hers and I squeezed it back.

And that was the moment we made it off the island.

Six months later

I got my notebook back pretty soon after we were rescued, but, for a long time, I didn't want to even look at it again. For ages, every time I thought about what had happened, I would get this rage boiling up inside of me. The unfairness of it all would twist my stomach. I'd have to move to get it out, to go for a walk or to dance. I couldn't stay still but I had to wait for my wrist to fully heal before I could do acrobatics.

But the truth is, the notebook was how they found us. It deserves to know the end of the story.

The storm that had extinguished my fire had caused a ship to go off route and it was waiting for the lane to be clear at the port before it headed there. While it waited, the crew spotted a life jacket and T-shirt floating in the sea and had thought it was a person, just like Vanna had hoped. They'd picked it up and found the notebook instead. They'd read it, realised where we were, called the police and then the police had come to find us.

When we got off the police boat on mainland Cambodia, we were met with flashes of cameras and news crews. And there standing amongst them were Mum, Dad and Olly. Seeing them again was one of the best moments of my entire life.

Mum gasped and ran over to me, followed by Dad and Olly.

The first thing Olly asked after we'd all hugged for ages was, 'Have you got chicken pox?'

I shook my head, confused, and he pointed to my bites. I'd forgotten my face and body were completely covered in red spots from the sandflies. I laughed and told him they were bites.

To my right I saw Bora holding Vanna in his arms.

'We're so lucky to have you back,' Mum said as she stroked my hair. 'We're so lucky the police found you.'

At the police station, we spilled everything that had happened. The police almost didn't believe me, even though they'd read my notebook, until I unwrapped Goldie and showed them a peek of her sleeping in my sling. Vanna drew a map of the island so that they knew exactly where to find the temple ruin headquarters and the smugglers who were hopefully still trapped there.

At the end, the police officer spoke to Mum and Dad. 'Your daughter has done something quite amazing. She's managed to uncover an international smuggling ring and catch two of their ringleaders in the process.'

'And find the gibbons,' I added.

'We've been trying to pin them down for years. We've gotten close but never been able to prove that it's them. And now we've caught them red-handed, thanks to you,' said the officer.

Mum smiled at me, glancing between me and the officer. 'That's my girl,' she said proudly, and kissed me on the cheek. 'My brave, clever girl.'

'It wasn't just me,' I said. 'It was Vanna too.'

When we came outside all the other police officers were looking and smiling at Goldie.

Later, the police returned with Crawler and Scratcher and a woman I didn't recognise in handcuffs. They'd manged to catch and rescue the two other gibbons, who were going to be transported to a wildlife sanctuary.

The next day, after my wrist had been X-rayed and bandaged, Bora organised for the gibbons to be transported to a sanctuary in the

North East of Cambodia. We drove with them, leaving the flat rice paddies behind us as we climbed up into lush green rolling hills. We passed wooden farmhouses, tuk-tuks filled with watermelons and whole villages on stilts connected by rope bridges. Bora told me all about gibbons, and how when Goldie was a grown-up her fur would turn from black to golden, so her name suited her perfectly. I asked him where Vanna was and he replied that she was still recovering at home. He didn't seem to want to talk about her but then he quietly said, 'You know, I couldn't be more grateful that you two are OK. I blame myself for you both getting involved in this mess,' and I knew instantly that he'd forgiven Vanna for helping the smugglers to begin with.

We entered through thick jungle along a dirt track to the wildlife sanctuary. We had to travel the last bit by boat, motoring along a river until we reached a thundering waterfall. When we passed a giant ibis, Bora said that it was good luck.

After spending the night in a wooden shack, I awoke to a familiar sound. It was our morning song, but instead of just Goldie, it was a whole chorus of gibbons. I took Goldie outside and she let out a squeal of excitement. I could tell that she recognised the trees. They were a different type to the ones on the island. *This* was her habitat.

'You go,' I said to her. She climbed up the nearest tree and sang along with the other gibbons. As the chorus filled the air, I felt like her song was finally complete. It was never meant to be sung alone.

'Will she be OK without me?' I asked Bora later.

'She was only in captivity for a week or two. She'll be fine,' said Bora. 'But the team will monitor her to make sure of it.'

I nodded, hoping that Bora was right. Goldie sang even when she was alone. She would be fine without me.

Although I wasn't sure if I would be OK without her.

I saw Vanna once more before I left.

We stood in front of each other.

She looked clean and smelled of fresh mango shampoo. She was still thinner than before the island, suntanned and sunburnt, with a cut down one cheek and scratched-up arms and legs, but her eyes sparkled, no longer dry and dull from the dehydration.

'Thanks for coming back to save me,' I said.

'Thanks for giving me a second chance,' she replied.

I smiled at her.

'Hey, why did you call the gibbon Goldie?'

she asked.

I shrugged. 'Her cheeks were sort of a gold colour. I knew straight away she was precious. Why?' I asked.

'It's what my name means,' said Vanna. 'Gold.'

'Maybe we were supposed to be on the island together,' I replied.

'I think so,' she said and we hugged. I hoped I would see her again.

When I first got home, I missed Goldie terribly. But I knew she was in her natural habitat, in her home, and I was thankful to be in mine. Back at school everything was so normal that it was almost as though being shipwrecked didn't happen. Except that the news about what had happened to me had made it to school. People asked me all sorts of questions.

'Did you get attacked by a shark?'

'Did you have to drink your own wee?'

'Did you eat frogs? They're a Cambodian delicacy.'

When I saw Sophia, she hugged me tightly. 'I just can't believe it,' she said.

I told Sophia how my acrobatics had saved Goldie.

'Well, *that* I can believe,' she said and we both laughed together.

It was hard adjusting to normal life again though. Whenever I went outside, cars and loud noises would make me jump and send my heart racing. My therapist explained that I was still in a state of *hyperarousal*, the same way I was on the island, when I was constantly on the lookout for snakes, food, or someone to rescue me. I was aware of threats around me – even though now there were no longer the same threats. My therapist said it was the way my mind was coping with the experience. He said none of it was my fault and it was all completely normal, which made me feel a bit better about it.

I remembered how the gibbon knew when she was in danger and when she wasn't, and I'm going to try and do the same thing. My therapist said it might help to have a kit of things that would help me feel safe, so I put together an emergency bag of matches and cereal bars and torches and batteries and a signal flare and whistle. My survival kit.

For a while I carried it everywhere, like a toddler with a floppy bunny. Now I don't need it any more, but I still do need a lot of time by myself. It took me a while to get used to being alone without Goldie.

The other day I climbed a tree in the garden and just sat in it all day, next to two squirrels who barked at me to get out. It wasn't the same as being on the island.

Olly stood below and called my name until I helped him climb up and he joined me and rested his head on my shoulder. That turned out to be all I needed.

I can sense that Mum and Dad are still scared to let me out of their sight but they're trying to allow me to carry on as normal.

It was two months later before I was given the all-clear to do acrobatics. Sophia and I practised our routine for another gymnastics competition that was coming up. I added in Goldie's signature move, running with her arms up then jumping from crouching and swinging.

I felt better after tumbling.

The only thing was Sophia kept asking me if I was OK all the time. She never used to do that. And I didn't feel she was pushing me as hard as she usually did during our sessions.

'You don't have to tiptoe around me,' I said to Sophia, as we put our shoes on after a practice. 'I'm still me.'

Maybe telling her that made all the difference. We had our best practice the next day. I did a new twist I didn't know that I could do.

A few weeks ago we performed our routine together on stage for the competition. Just before my finishing routine, I looked up and saw Mum, Dad and Olly smiling at me in the crowd. I took a big run up and tumbled through the air. And for a split second, I was back on the island, following Goldie through the trees, singing as we went.

Up until that moment, I had been wishing the whole thing had never happened. But that was when I realised: I wouldn't change anything about getting shipwrecked. I've learnt so much from it. About myself, and what I'm truly capable of.

Vanna and I have been emailing. She sent me the photo Bora took of us all that day we first met at the beach and I printed it out and pinned it to my wardrobe. Vanna also told me what happened to the smugglers. Crawler and Scratcher gave up the names of the other people who had been in on the gibbon smuggling. It included some police officers and also the government official, Mr Sok, who Bora and Mum had interviewed. That was how the smuggling ring had operated for so long without being caught – they had people in high places helping them. Mr Sok had been using gibbon bone balm to help his wife's arthritis. He said that it was the only thing helping her.

Soon Vanna's going to come and visit me. I can't wait.

Mum kept all the newspaper articles that were written while I was lost on the island. My favourite was the last one.

*TWO GIRLS UNCOVER INTERNATIONAL
SMUGGLING RING*

*After being washed up on separate islands, two girls not
only survived without food and water, but eventually came
together to uncover an international smuggling ring. The girls
showed bravery, courage and unbelievable strength.*

*Some officials have been caught up in the ongoing
investigation . . .*

There's only one last page left in this notebook
and there's one last thing you need to know
before I go. Together the North and South
Islands are being renamed Gibbon Island. The
government is going to keep it uninhabited and
turn it into an eco-sanctuary. Apparently the
giant clams in the waters there are endangered
and it's one of the only places they still live.
People will be able to do day visits though, and
watch the dolphins. Bora and Vanna have started
the tours. Maybe one day I'll go on one of them.

People are surprised when I say that I want to go back to visit one day – but even after everything that happened, I wouldn't change it. I can almost think about the experience fondly now. It was my love for Goldie that gave me the courage to survive on that island. I survived that, so I know I can overcome anything.

And whenever I'm feeling scared, I whistle our song and feel hope inside my heart, leaping and acrobatic, just like Goldie.

Author Note

In 2007, I visited Cambodia and travelled by boat to a small, undeveloped island off the coast. I'd only planned on staying there a few days, but on the third day a storm raged and the ocean became too treacherous for the boat to return and collect me. I ended up getting stuck on the island for two weeks. Thankfully, it wasn't uninhabited, and I had a leaking wooden hut to stay in, which I shared with screeching frogs and once a tree snake. Although there was no electricity, I had food, water, shelter and company. I spent a lot of my time there imagining what it would be like to have to survive on an island without any of those comforts.

Eventually the boat showed up – a tiny open dinghy with an outboard motor – and I climbed aboard with two drivers. As we headed into open waters, the wind and waves picked up.

Our tiny boat would rise into the air on the top of huge waves before crashing down and rocking from side to side, water splashing onboard. Every time, the outboard motor would cut out and I'd wonder if I might actually end up getting shipwrecked on one of the uninhabited islands that we passed.

After what felt like hours, the mainland came into view, but the currents were too strong to get close to shore. I pulled my backpack on, jumped off the boat, and swam with all my might to the beach. Gibbon Island is a fictional place, but it was inspired by this experience. Cambodia, with its crumbling temples, jungle and endangered howling gibbons that fill the trees, has always been a setting I've wanted to write about.

Last year, I learnt that over the past decade 1700 environmental activists have been murdered. Many were people trying to protect the environment they live in from being destroyed. Thirteen of them were environmental journalists investigating stories. This struck a chord with me. I always tell young people that you should write about the things you care about and feel passionately about, and immediately this became a subject I wanted to explore in a story. Writing has always been my way of trying to understand the world around me. One of the things I've learned is that you can find hope and courage in the most unlikely of places.

Acknowledgements

A huge thank you to everyone involved in creating this book.

To Rob Biddulph, thank you for the beautiful illustrations including the stunning cover and amazing map! Lark and the gibbon are gorgeous.

So many thanks to my editor, Lena McCauley, for being alongside me at every stage of this book – from finding the right structure for the voice, to shaping the story arc, to making the words sing.

To my agent, Sallyanne Sweeney, for your continued encouragement and friendship, thank you. It's been such a joy to finally be able to have in person cups of tea and even a trip to the zoo!

To Steve Voake, thank you for helping me get to the heart of the story at the very beginning of this idea and your editorial advice. It allowed me to finish that very first draft.

To Ruth Girmatsion, thank you for taking the book through all the final stages and patiently reading my many last-minute tweaks!

Thanks to Genevieve Herr for your copyedit and valuable insight about many things including the reality of carrying objects whilst treading water in the ocean. I spent my summer in the sea in Cornwall experimenting and still came away wondering the same thing!

To proofreader Adele Brimacombe, thank you.

A huge thanks to everyone at Hachette Children's Group, the wonderful design team, the marketing and publicity team, and everyone else involved. It's a joy to be part of the Hachette family.

Thanks to my family and friends, especially to my mum, Anya, my mother in law, Anne, my sisters Olivia, Rachel and Hazel, and husband Jonathan, for your continued support and taking care of a little bean so I could sneak away and write.

Thank you to all the young readers I've met, especially Indie, Katie and Evie. You are all stars.

Thanks to everyone who's working to protect the world we love and the biodiversity within it. You inspired much of this story.